The Pitards

GEORGES SIMENON

The Pitards

Translated by DAVID BELLOS

PENGUIN BOOKS

PENGUIN CLASSICS

UK | USA | Canada | Ireland | Australia
India | New Zealand | South Africa

Penguin Books is part of the Penguin Random House group of companies
whose addresses can be found at global.penguinrandomhouse.com.

First published in French as *Les Pitard* by Gallimard 1935
This translation first published 2017
001

Set in 12.04/15 pt Dante MT Std
Typeset by Jouve (UK), Milton Keynes
Printed in Great Britain by Clays Ltd, St Ives plc

ISBN: 978–0–241–29989–0

The Pitards

1.

In the shipping news column in the *Journal de Rouen*, under 'Departures':

'*Tonnerre-de-Dieu*, under Captain Lannec, to Hamburg, with 500 tonnes mixed cargo . . .'

From Rouen pilot station to Villequier pilot station, by telephone:

'In two hours you'll have the *Tonnerre-de-Dieu* with 3m50 freeboard. Tell the bos'n his cousin from Paimpol has just turned up and sends greetings . . .'

'Ahoy! The *Picardie* we told you was coming upriver has anchored at La Vacquerie instead.'

'Storm brewing over your way?'

'Blowing up nicely.'

For the third time, Mathilde Lannec put her hand to her mouth and deposited on the edge of her plate a blob of greenish string from the runner beans she'd been chewing.

Lannec pretended not to notice his wife's behaviour or the sigh she gave to express her view of the meal, but a moment later he couldn't help exchanging a glance with Mathias, his chief engineer, who'd been as quiet as the grave throughout dinner.

There were four of them at the mess table: Mathias, Émile Lannec, his wife Mathilde and Paul, the radio operator with a glass eye, who was barely more talkative than his colleague.

Moinard, the chief mate, was on watch on the bridge, and

because the rain was coming down in sheets the second mate had been sent to the forecastle as lookout man.

'You ought to have stronger lights put in,' Mathilde decreed as the beef stew was served.

To tell the truth, the mess room was poorly lit. You could even stare at the yellow filaments in the bulbs without hurting your eyes. Lannec shot a glance at the chief engineer, who scratched his head.

'Sorry, but I don't have any other lightbulbs on board.'

'Remember to buy some when we get to Hamburg.'

'I'm afraid the wiring won't take higher wattage.'

Madame Lannec fell silent, but her frown said what she was thinking. Were they trying to make fun of her? Not really. But something of that sort hung in the air.

Her husband was in a strange mood. She had not often seen him so playful or, more exactly, detached.

For instance, when she was staring at a glass smeared with finger marks, Lannec called out:

'Campois!'

Campois was the steward. As he was from Fécamp, he was called 'le Fécampois', Campois for short.

'Take care to wipe the glassware, won't you?'

He said it so gently and ironically that it sounded more like a compliment than a reprimand.

The radiator was scorching hot. Now and again the engineer listened hard to the rhythm of the pistons, which made the bulkheads rattle.

Lannec, on the other hand, pricked up his ears at the grating sound of the wheelhouse chains.

'We're heading into the Heurtanville bend,' he declared.

Or else:

'We're abreast of the Meule light.'

He couldn't see a thing. The curtains were drawn over the

rain-streaked portholes, and the atmosphere was so humid that drops of water ran down the enamel-painted bulkheads like beads of sweat.

Because Madame Lannec was present, the one-eyed radio operator and the chief engineer put on collars and ties for dinner, but Lannec couldn't bring himself to dress up. His thick blue worsted pea-jacket was open over his shirt, showing up the pot belly that his sturdy appetite had given him. He had his elbows on the table and was leaning forwards to eat his soup.

There was a familiar odour in the air, a compound of cooking smells, engine oil, and the sweat of the four men whose quarters opened directly on to the mess room.

'I'll be back in five minutes,' Lannec said as he stood up, grabbing his oilskins on his way out.

They were approaching Villequier. The freighter had slowed down to take on a new river pilot. Despite his oilskins, Captain Lannec was soaked through by the icy rain by the time he got to the bridge.

Moinard, the first mate, was standing stock still at the wheel in the gloom. The departing pilot was buttoning up his oilskins.

'A glass of calvados?'

Lannec went into the chart house and filled two glasses.

'Who's taking over?'

'Fatty Pérault.'

'Still on the job, at his age?'

They were following the Seine downstream, but the river couldn't be seen. Behind the darting raindrops there was just more rain, more wetness, and somewhere in all that dampness were two or three lights as hazy as eyes weeping tears.

'Cheers! Another dram?'

A launch came alongside in the dark. The pilot went down the rope ladder, and another gleaming shape came over the railing and up to the bridge.

'Is it stormy out there?' Lannec asked the new pilot, whose job was to lead the ship to the open sea.

'A fair swell.'

Lannec put off going back down to the mess room. He felt better up here, behind the rain-swept window of the bridge lit only by the halo of the compass light.

He liked to make out the dim sight of Moinard at the helm, standing there like a statue with his face right up to the windscreen as he concentrated on the course ahead, alongside the river pilot who was filling his pipe and muttering, 'Left hand down, and look out for the fishing boat that must be somewhere over there . . .'

Lannec went up to Moinard and sighed:

'You know, things aren't great down below!'

Moinard didn't respond, obviously. He never did. He carried on staring straight ahead, but that didn't mean he hadn't heard.

'Has anyone seen my cigarette lighter?'

He went back into the chart house, which contained just a sofa and a table covered in charts, switched on the light, found his lighter and came across a piece of squared paper which he had to put under the light to read.

'Moinard!' he called out.

'Yes, skipper.'

'Have you been in here?'

'No, skipper.'

'Did you see anyone come in here?'

'Nobody has been in the chart house.'

Lannec grunted, shoved the piece of paper in his pocket and went back down to the mess room.

'You'd do well to go to bed,' he said to his wife. 'I have to take my turn on the bridge.'

The chief engineer had left the table and gone back to the engine room. The radio operator was hovering politely, not sure if he should stay or go. A green baize drape had replaced the tablecloth so as to make the mess room look more like a lounge.

'Will there be high seas?' Mathilde asked once she was alone with her husband.

'Not very. There'll be more of a swell when we get into the Channel.'

'You seem to like the idea.'

'Do I? Not at all.'

'Admit it, you're angry at having me on board!'

'Of course not . . .'

The protest was no more than lukewarm. He gave his wife a kiss on her forehead as he pushed open the door to her cabin.

'If you need anything, just ring the bell.'

'To summon that boy with the dirty hands?'

'I'll tell him to wash his hands.'

'I could barely eat a thing.'

'Obviously.'

'Obviously what?'

'Nothing!'

Or everything! Her idea of living on board was madness itself. She'd been married to him for two years and had had plenty of time to get used to his absences, since he'd never stopped sailing ships.

But now he had a ship of his own! And that was the reason! He wasn't just a skipper now. He was a ship owner, so she'd insisted on coming along.

'Good night.'

'You too.'

He was alone at last. He scratched his stubbly cheeks and poured himself a glass of water. He had a hangover. Last night, at the Café de Paris in Rouen, a few of them had drunk to the new freighter or rather, to the freighter that had changed owners.

It was an old English steamer that had already been at sea for sixty years under the name of *Busiris*.

'What are we going to call her?' Lannec wondered when he bought her. 'I'd like to find a name that isn't ordinary, goddammit.'

'Call it the *Tonnerre-de-Dieu*!'

'*Tonnerre de Dieu*' was his favourite swear word.

It was another one of the evenings when they had all had a skinful. Lannec thumped the table with his fist.

'Done!'

'Bet you won't go through with it!'

'Bet you I will!'

He did not back down even in the face of his wife's and mother-in-law's tearful protests.

'I think I have a right to be heard,' his mother-in-law objected.

And she did, alas. A hundred times alas! Lannec and Moinard had gone into partnership to purchase the ship, but they hadn't had quite enough to clinch the deal in cash. The bank that loaned them the balance required a guarantee from someone with visible assets.

Lannec's wife's mother, Madame Pitard, owned two residential buildings in Caen and a seaside villa at Riva-Bella.

Her signature had done its job, and that's why she considered herself to be part-owner of the *Tonnerre-de-Dieu*.

Who knows, maybe she had advised her daughter to live on board so as to keep an eye on the two men?

Lannec was gargling, though still in his oilskins, when he saw the second mate come in. Monsieur Gilles was a young man from Paris who wore a pencil moustache.

'Is the weather clearing?'

'Not a lot. I've come down to make my bed.'

Another complication! Mathilde Lannec wanted her own quarters, and so everything had to be turned inside out. She got Moinard's cabin, Moinard got Monsieur Gilles', and

Monsieur Gilles was reduced to bunking on the bench in the mess room.

He had come down with his mattress and sheets and began to make up his bed.

'All right, I'll go back up on deck,' Lannec sighed.

The *Tonnerre-de-Dieu* was a good ship, everyone had agreed last night. They don't make ships like that any more; nowadays they skimp on the quality of the materials. Lannec even liked its narrow funnel, as it made the ship something of a curio.

On the stairway he bumped into Campois and winked at him. He had second thoughts once he'd gone past, and turned round to say:

'You know something? You'll have to wash your hands more often now.'

Lannec was a short man with a heavy chin – he was a Breton, after all – and small, mischievous eyes. Once he was on deck he leaned on the railing and made out the Courval lighthouse. A huge tanker was on its way down the Seine in front of the *Tonnerre-de-Dieu*. Up on the bridge Moinard must have stretched his arm out to the fog horn handle, because a long blast followed by two shorter ones could be heard.

That meant they were going to pass the tanker on the port side.

'Who ever could have written that?' Lannec grunted as he scrunched the piece of squared paper in his pocket.

He went through the friends he'd been with the night before. Friends? Not exactly. Just people you can have a beer with, like Bernheim, the shipbroker who'd got him the freight, the deputy harbourmaster, a tug master and a customs inspector . . .

'You start with one old ship, *tonnerre de Dieu*, and you can end up with a whole fleet, like Fabre or Worms!'

He wasn't stoked up by the drink so much as by being with a group of fellows in a well-lit café, by the chink of crockery and the waiter's conniving smiles. Lannec felt he was turning into a superman. He could be heard all over the room, and the more he talked the more enthusiastic he got.

'Let me tell you! My father was just a fisherman on a cod trawler. I went to sea at the age of fifteen, but look at me now . . .'

Lannec shrugged. It's always embarrassing to remember what you said on occasions of that kind. The rain on his face was doing him good. Before going up to the bridge he stuck his head into the engine room, saw deep down below splendid steel parts in silent motion, and smelled a pleasing odour of hot engine oil. Mathias, the chief engineer, was talking to the lookout man.

'All hunky dory?'

'Hunky dory it is.'

Would anyone have dared to sabotage *his* engine? He got up to the bridge and stood next to the pilot, who had only fifteen more minutes on board.

'A shot of calvados?'

It was a ritual they went through without thinking. Lannec filled two glasses, like he had done before. Moinard shot him a glance that meant to say, 'May I go below decks?'

Moinard was a good guy, he really was. He did his job as chief mate just the way he would if he hadn't been half-owner of the ship.

'Wait a bit.'

The Seine was widening into the estuary. Despite the curtain of rain you could sense the glow over Le Havre, and there were more and more fishing boats around the banks, where there were shoals of sprats.

'What are they saying about me in Rouen since I became an owner?'

'That you're a lucky man!' the pilot replied, taking the wheel himself and giving it a quarter turn.

'Are some people jealous?'

'There are always jealous people.'

'Who, in particular?'

'You know, I don't pay much attention to that kind of talk . . .'

'A last dram?'

They clinked glasses. The pilot sounded his whistle to summon the launch to take him off.

'I hear you're taking your wife. Like some English captains do. Maybe there's a good side to it . . .'

They were thinking of something quite different as they watched out for the few lights that shone through the watery fog.

'There they are! Slow astern.'

Moinard operated the wireless. The boat slowed down in the current, and then there were voices in the dark and a slight bump against the hull.

'Be seeing you!' the pilot said as he held out his hand for a shake.

'See you soon!'

A few more manoeuvres, and the *Tonnerre-de-Dieu* was on her own. Lannec gave the order to go full steam ahead.

He was going out to sea, for real, on his own boat! He blinked at the Hève light, which he'd spotted so many times before, and some of last night's enthusiasm came back to him.

'Georges!'

He didn't often call Moinard by his first name.

'Some bastard has tried to play a trick on me.'

As he said that he handed over the piece of paper he'd found in the chart house.

'Have a read of that.'

The little light shone once again over the charts. Lannec checked they were on the right course and that there was nothing ahead of them, except for a liner all lit up in the far distance.

'What do you think? Must be some idiot who wants to give us a scare, right?'

Moinard turned over the scrap in his fingers. The message on it had been written in crayon:

Don't try to be too clever. A person who knows what he's saying is telling you that the *Tonnerre-de-Dieu* will not reach safe haven. That person sends greetings to you and says hallo to Mathilde.

'He knows my wife,' Lannec observed. That detail hadn't struck him before.

However, she did not live in Rouen, but in Caen, where her mother had given the young couple an apartment in one of the buildings she owned.

'A practical joke, right?'

'You never know,' Moinard sighed, seeming not overly concerned.

'What could they have done? Sabotage the engine?'

He suddenly felt fond of his old ship now he saw her as being under threat. He talked about her different parts as if he were speaking of a living being.

'The rudder? We would already have noticed something. And the hull is as tough as they come . . .'

He gave a sudden jump and then burst out laughing. He'd had a fright on hearing a noise so strange from the forward hatch that at first he hadn't realized what it was.

It was a cow mooing!

'I'd forgotten . . .'

They had two on board, a pair of buxom Normandy cows for delivery in Hamburg, tethered on the open deck. A sailor had done his best to pitch a canvas awning over the animals, but even so rivulets of rain ran down their black-and-white flanks.

And now they were mooing, perhaps from fright at the mysterious sea.

'Tell me it's a joke. Isn't it?'

Now they had left estuarial waters the ship got into its usual sway, and waves started breaking over the bow.

'I bet my wife will get up.'

He wasn't wrong. Down below, Mathilde opened her cabin door, in her nightdress, looked around for someone in the ill-lit mess room and finally espied the light-coloured sheets covering Monsieur Gilles as he lay in his bunk.

'Are we at sea?'

Monsieur Gilles was already asleep. He just sighed and turned over in his bed.

'Émile! . . .' Mathilde called out in a half-whisper.

She listened, heard no response and went back into her cabin, but she could not get back to sleep for an hour. She kept the light on. She kept on staring at the enamelled bulkheads and found they were covered in stains.

'It all needs a good scrub . . .'

The red leaf-pattern carpet on the floor was dirty too, with dark stains of who knows what. Then to cap it all was the smell, she would never get used to it. The bulkheads must have been not properly sealed, which would explain the odours of burned oil and coal.

'Do you mind staying on watch for a moment longer?' Lannec asked Moinard.

He wasn't keen on doing what he had to do, but there was no standing in the way of it. First he went down to the engine room, where there was only one engineer, because Mathias had gone to bed.

'You didn't notice anything unusual, did you?'

'No, I didn't, captain. Except that the oil we took on in Rouen is too light. We'll get through more of it.'

Lannec looked at the pistons and the dynamo and slipped into the boiler room, where there were two men sitting next to the coal stack.

'All in order?'

'Aye, aye, captain.'

Ice-cold air laden with raindrops was coming down the

ventilation shaft, so that as you walked past you went from hellish heat to an unexpected patch of cool.

Lannec was about to turn around but decided to slip through a manhole and cast an eye over the long tunnel that housed the transmission shaft. Not a drop of water inside. The shaft was going round nicely. No leakage from the gland.

Before going back up to the bridge Lannec opened the mess-room door, noticed Monsieur Gilles sleeping and saw light coming from under his wife's cabin door. He could have gone in to give her a kiss but preferred to go on his way.

'Must be a joker!' he said to himself one more time.

He smiled at the cows staring at him with frightened eyes, shook out his oilskins and went to stand next to Moinard.

'A joker!' he said, aloud.

'Can I stand down?'

'Goodnight! Try not to wake up my wife. She must have dropped off with the light on.'

Then he filled his pipe with tobacco and took stock of the horizon. The Hève light was moving abeam, and the glare of the Antifer lighthouse was already in range.

Then it would be Fécamp, then Saint-Valéry, Dieppe, Boulogne . . . The ship's bell rang midnight, and a shadow glided noiselessly along the bridge to take over the wheel while the retiring steersman mumbled as if in a dream:

'North by north-east.'

'North by north-east,' the newcomer said in the same tone.

With his pipe crackling, Lannec put his forehead to the rainy windshield and felt the presence of the imperturbable steersman behind him.

Then there was a loud noise of something hitting the deck. One of the cows had finally decided to lie down.

2.

It was nearly eleven in the morning before they caught sight of Dungeness, the first foreland on the English coast. The rain had cleansed the sky, which was now pale blue. All morning they'd had the white cliffs of Normandy to starboard.

Lannec, who had gone to bed at six, came up to the bridge in his clogs and braces, unshaven and bleary-eyed.

Campois hadn't needed to wake him up or to tell him where they were. One glance at the English coast, a second glance at France, and he motioned to give the wheel a turn to port.

The *Tonnerre-de-Dieu* was sailing into where the sandbanks were – The Ridge, Bullock Bank, Les Ridens, Vergoyer, and other unseen dangers that obstruct most of the Dover Strait.

Monsieur Gilles was on watch, all neat and smartly dressed from the crack of dawn.

'What was all that noise about?' Lannec asked as he leaned forwards over the charts.

'I don't know. I didn't hear anything.'

The skipper walked over to the railing and yelled:

'Campois! My coffee, *tonnerre de Dieu!*'

It was cold. Lannec stamped up and down the deck to get warm and kept an eye on the white horses that showed where the first sandbanks were. As for Moinard, he was still asleep. An engineer had set up a vice on deck and was grinding a metal part, which made a screech.

'Have the cattle been seen to?'

The deck was still wet, as was everything you could touch, and despite the clear sky it felt as if the air itself hadn't yet dried out.

'What's been passing?'

'Two German ships, and some English coalers.'

Lannec was getting impatient. The steward had never taken so long to bring up his coffee, and when he finally came he looked even glummer than usual.

He was a thin, ageless lad who seemed to have no life of his own, coming and going with a look of resignation on his face, unruffled by the blows of fate and not even trying to ward them off, as if it were in the natural order of things for them to rain down upon him.

'Where've you been?'

'In the galley, sir.'

Lannec glanced without thinking at Campois' hands. They were crimson from having been scrubbed with a brush.

'What was the racket I heard this morning?'

'I don't know, sir.'

'Is my wife up?'

The steward nodded with such an eloquent expression in his eyes that Lannec couldn't help laughing. He sipped at his coffee but kept his eye on the horizon all the time.

'What time did she call?'

'At eight, to ask for her *café au lait*.'

Lannec guessed that wasn't the whole story.

'And then?'

'Then she called for hot water.'

Monsieur Gilles was pretending not to listen in, but he was smiling as well as he looked the other way.

'Then?'

'She called me again for hot water and soft soap.'

'Soft soap?'

'Yes, soap and floor cloths. She made me scrub down the cabin bulkheads.'

Each sentence had to be winkled out of him.

'That's all?'

Campois didn't answer. He stood there waiting for the empty cup, looking distracted and miserable at the same time. Monsieur Gilles claimed he was the picture of a sickly seminarist.

'So what else happened?'

The pause was much longer this time. Campois was reluctant to open his mouth.

'During the night . . .' he stammered at long last.

The steward's responsibilities on board were quite complex, because he was head waiter, valet and assistant cook rolled into one. As he wasn't at all greedy – in fact, he hardly ate anything – he'd been made guardian of the store room, which was where he slept.

'Out with it, you cretin!'

'The ghost came and took a whole ham,' he blurted out at high speed, as if each word was being chased by the other.

'Eh? What's that nonsense?'

They were interrupted by Mathilde Lannec, who appeared at the top of the ladder, looking suspicious and braced against a hostile environment.

'I couldn't find you in your cabin,' she said to her husband. 'Are we past Boulogne?'

'Not yet. It's over there, beneath those four radio masts. Wait a minute while I clear up this story about a ghost . . .'

'A ghost?'

'Speak up, Campois. Don't stand there like an idiot. What ghost?'

'The ghost of the *Busiris*. When the ship still had that name there was already a ghost on board, it was an English ghost . . .'

'Upon my word! And who told you that?'

Campois looked around with a fearful glance and then mumbled:

'Everyone. The bos'n . . .'

The bos'n was on deck at that moment, attempting to milk the cows.

'Ahoy! Come up here!' Lannec shouted down to him.

He put on a stern face, but laughter twinkled in his small eyes. Now and again he winked at his wife and Monsieur Gilles.

'So now it seems there's a ghost on my ship, and that you've seen it!'

'Last night, in the store room . . .'

'Dressed in a white sheet, of course?'

Campois nodded his head. The bos'n clambered up and waited to be addressed, pretending to be thinking about something else.

'And he spoke English,' Campois added.

'And you say he made off with a ham?'

'The biggest.'

'English ghosts must like ham,' Lannec muttered dreamily. 'You can stand down, Campois. I'll deal with this.'

He broke off to alter course slightly, filled his first pipe of the day and pulled up his pea-jacket collar over his half-open shirt.

'Bos'n!'

'Aye, skipper.'

'You will give an order to the ghost to put the ham back in its place tonight.'

'But . . .'

'And you will tell him, in addition, that if this is not done, I will put him ashore in Hamburg without a centime in pay.'

'Honestly, I swear . . .'

'Now go and milk your cows.'

He was in a good mood and stood in front of Mathilde to look her up and down.

He had a pretty wife. Her soft brown wavy hair framed a face that, although not regular, was very youthful, and her body too was attractively young. Could you criticize her for the hint of harshness in the shape of her mouth? She got it from her mother; it was the same in all the Pitards whose portraits Lannec had seen.

'Sleep well? Gilles, you can stand down.'

'You might as well say I didn't sleep at all.'

Just behind them stood the steersman, that unalterable presence on the bridge, but he was so still that they didn't take any notice of him being there.

'You'll get used to it,' Lannec said jovially. 'You feel disoriented to begin with   '

'I'll never get used to filth! I don't need to change, but this boat does! This morning . . .'

'I know.'

'What do you know?'

'You commandeered Campois and got him to scrub down the bulkheads in your cabin. Only that means the potatoes will be late . . .'

'Do I not have the right to make use of the servant?'

It seemed to Lannec that a faint smile could be made out on the face of the steersman after all.

'So you do, my darling. What I was saying . . .'

'Aren't you going to shave?'

'I've just come up on bridge after four hours' sleep, at the most.'

He had spent the night up here on his own alongside the steersman, ceaselessly watching the same lights looming in the dark. He was frowning now because there was a sou'wester rising. It was still imperceptible but it would soon be strong enough to raise a swell over the banks.

'What's happening about the ghost?'

Before answering he pointed to the bos'n, who was red in

the face as he carried on trying to draw out one of the cows' udders. The bos'n was even shorter and squatter than Lannec, and his broken nose made him look like a cartoon idiot.

'What does he do on board?'

'He's in charge of the crew and sometimes does a watch. Who's the ghost? He is!'

'I don't understand.'

'That bumpkin knows that Campois is as superstitious as an old maid. He spun him a yarn about the boat having a ghost on board and took advantage of him by slipping into the glory-hole last night and stealing a whole ham. Campois didn't even think of raising the alarm . . .'

'He's a thief!'

'He's a bos'n, and a first-rate one too.'

'Are you going to throw him out the door?'

He smiled at the word 'door', and at Mathilde's indignation.

'He'll put the ham back tonight.'

'And that's all?'

'That's all.'

'So you let people steal from you . . .'

'Of course not, since the ham will be put back.'

'They'll steal something else . . .'

He patted her on the shoulder affectionately.

'Off you go! You can't understand . . .'

'Where am I supposed to go?'

'The mess room, your cabin, wherever.'

Once Mathilde had left, Lannec poured himself the glass of calvados that he drank every morning after his first coffee and without thinking reread the handwritten note he'd found the previous night.

'Bloody joker!'

The wind had overtaken the *Tonnerre-de-Dieu* already, and the sea, which had been calm just a short while earlier, was now breaking into white horses and was turning from a greenish colour to a fairly ominous grey.

'To starboard,' he said to the man at the wheel. 'We're just abreast of Vergoyer.'

He was smoking gently, drawing very small puffs on his pipe. He went into the chart house again to get a knitted woollen scarf and wiped his dripping nose with the back of his hand.

He felt irrationally inclined to walk about, wave his arms and talk to someone, which he did not do very often.

'It'll be rough after Dover,' he said to the steersman, who didn't answer, since it wasn't his job to do so.

Lannec poured himself a second glass of calvados and leaned over to look at the cows now that the bos'n had left them in peace.

The air was clear, for now. The cliffs of Normandy were growing faint, but the outlines of the chimneys and cranes of Boulogne could be seen in sharper relief. Here and there a stubby trawler laboured through the waves.

'The joker!'

He wasn't thinking about it. He was just about as light-hearted as usual, because, overall, he was a good-humoured man, especially in the morning. They'd be making an average of eight knots and more because of the following current. The *Tonnerre-de-Dieu* was sailing very respectably for a ship sixty years old.

All the same Lannec was walking around, cleaning his pipe, filling it again and spitting in the sea instead of standing still, as he usually did. There was an emptiness inside him, something very subtle he could not quite grasp, a worry, perhaps, or a foreboding.

Not even! Just a slight stomach cramp, nothing more. Was he just a bit hungry? He had some sausage brought up. He chewed on it while still smoking his pipe.

He was wrong, obviously, but he couldn't resist it. He needed to be jolly. And the sight of his wife when he went down to the mess room put him into laughing mood.

A beam of sunlight coming through the porthole put a halo round Mathilde's head. The table was laid for six, but Mathilde was on her own. With her elbows on the tablecloth and her chin in her hands, she looked moody.

'They rang a while ago,' she said.

'That was the first bell. Listen! They're just ringing the second . . .'

Monsieur Gilles was on watch, so this time Moinard came to table. He bowed so solemnly to Mathilde that Lannec burst out laughing again.

'First rate! I now give you permission to kiss the lady's hand!'

Mathilde gave him a dirty look that he deflected by turning to the one-eyed radio operator, who put his head down and his nose into his plate.

'He's got a crush on her!' Lannec thought to himself. 'No doubt about it. Our Paul is in love with my wife, and is blushing like a girl.'

The chief mate unfolded his napkin with unparalleled ceremoniousness.

'Well, shipmates, seems like we're all starving!'

He said that just to say something, because he was happy and wanted to see happy faces around him.

'But I'm not hungry.'

The words came from Mathilde. Lannec frowned for a moment and was about to respond but bit off a chunk of bread instead.

Campois had never been so glum. You could see that Madame Lannec scared the daylights out of him and was making him clumsy. When he dropped a fork, picked it up and put it back on the table, Mathilde said:

'A clean one.'

He didn't understand.

'A clean what?'

'She's telling you to fling another fork on the floor, you nit-wit!' Lannec shouted.

It just came to him, but nobody else laughed. His wife turned towards him with a steely glance.

'Listen, dearest . . .'

He realized he was making matters worse, that things were on a downhill slide, but he couldn't stop himself.

'If you carry on harassing our Campois, he'll go and complain to his ghost. Cheer up, for God's sake! It's a fine life on the ocean wave . . .'

When he got excited he couldn't be calmed. He turned to the radio operator.

'What's the forecast, Paul?'

'Low pressure over Ireland . . . High seas in the North Sea . . .'

'What was I telling you? Everything is fine!'

'Do you think so?'

'It could be a lot worse.'

He was running out of ideas but didn't know how to extricate himself. The others ate without talking; Mathilde was tense and on the verge of having a tantrum.

'You see, my dearest, it's best to get a real battering the first time round. It'll give you your sea legs, and after that . . .'

'I'd prefer you to shut up. You're a fool.'

'Thanks for the compliment!'

'You're welcome.'

The radio operator didn't know where to look. Moinard was eating twice as much as usual, to keep up appearances.

'Campois! Come here.'

Lannec didn't know what he was going to do, but he couldn't stand the silence.

'Show me your hands! When we get to Hamburg, ask me for fifty centimes so you can buy a nail file.'

At that point Mathilde stood up with composure, went to her cabin and closed the door behind her.

'So there you are,' Lannec said.

He was furious and relieved at the same time. He was quite fond of his wife. He wished her no ill. All the same, there she was, in the middle of the mess room, a Pitard through and through!

Because there was a Pitard way of sitting down, a Pitard way of helping yourself to mustard and cutting up your meat and a Pitard way of staring straight through you!

'I'm not hungry any more,' he muttered, pushing his plate away and then filling his pipe. 'What do you think, Georges?'

He knew his wife was listening from behind her door. He spoke loud, on purpose. Moinard just shrugged his shoulders.

'Did I say anything wrong? I was in a good mood, I cracked a joke, and then . . .'

He rose from the table and went up on deck with leaden steps, as if to make his weight felt. If she was going to spoil all the fun he was having in owning his own boat . . . !

The sky was clouding over and turning the same grey colour as the sea, and a Newhaven–Dieppe steamer with crowds of passengers on deck passed by half a mile away. It was the time of day when Lannec usually took two hours off to rest. All the same he would wait until the other officers had finished their meal and left the mess room.

When he went back down, Campois was clearing the table. Lannec said nothing but stood at the porthole, drumming his fingers on the pane. The steward got the point and hurried up so much that he broke a glass.

'Joker!' the captain grumbled.

His quarters were on the right, but he didn't go in. He carried on waiting until the steward had left and then locked the outside door, which he never did. He went up to the door of his wife's cabin.

'Mathilde!'

No answer. But she wasn't asleep yet, he could hear noises in the cabin.

'Open up. I have to talk to you.'

'I'm listening.'

'Not like this. Open the door for a minute . . .'

Something like a smile came back to his face, and a lustful thought made his upper lip curl. It struck him that they hadn't even had a kiss since they'd been on board their own ship!

'Open the door, Mathilde!'

He put on a soft voice, leaned down to the keyhole and heard footsteps approaching.

'Don't be mean! I want to tell you that . . .'

He'd forgotten the incident at lunchtime already. That was the past! He was ready to take his wife in his arms.

'Open up, quickly.'

The bolt was drawn, the door opened a few inches, and in the gap there was Mathilde, looking stern.

'What's the matter?' she uttered.

His smile froze on his face. He made an effort nonetheless and stammered:

'Don't be cross. I promise you . . .'

The door was shut and bolted, and Lannec heard shoes fall to the ground. He raised his fist. For an instant that fist was on the point of hitting the door, but it carried on further up until it met the gimbal light that was used when the electricity was out. It had a green shade.

Lannec grasped its mounting, paused for a second, then tugged on it as hard as he could. He had to try twice, as it was firmly fixed to the bulkhead.

It made a thunderous noise in the mess room. Outside, there was alarm, presumably from Campois, who didn't know what disaster had befallen the ship.

Lannec for his part went into his cabin, shut the door and lay down on his bunk fully dressed.

For a while he didn't pay any attention to what was going on on the other side of the partition. Once quiet returned he could hear his wife's voice and realized that she was helping the steward repair or take stock of the damage.

3.

He slept for two hours and by five p.m. he was seated in the mess room by the light of the now shadeless gimbal, which had been put back on the wall. Because it was a ritual action, Campois put Lannec's bowl of coffee on the table with its green baize cover now on it without saying a word.

Just as Eastern soothsayers can fall into a trance by gazing at a crystal ball, Lannec, like servants and housekeepers, had the capacity to abstract his mind entirely over a bowl of coffee.

It was a huge earthenware bowl, half an inch thick. He poured condensed milk into it himself from a tin with two holes in it.

At this point he was still drowsy, halfway between sleep and waking. He was yawning, and his legs were numb. The smell of his hot, sweet drink chased away another smell that also had its place in the unchanging order of his days – the smell of the bunk he'd just left. He would never have dared admit this to anyone, but when he lay down for his afternoon nap he enjoyed that smell, like a horse happy to be back in its stable, and when he spent a few days ashore, he was disoriented by sleeping in another bed, even if it was his wife's.

'Campois!'

He didn't raise his voice because he knew the steward was nearby.

'Has the wind changed?'

Even dreaming over his milky coffee didn't stop him from

following the ship's progress. Even when he'd been asleep he'd registered that the wind had slackened and given way to squalls of rain drumming on the portholes.

Now he was lending his ear to the rush of sea on the hull, and the sound of the waves told him there was an upwind.

'North-west,' Campois confirmed.

Night had just fallen. The two electric lightbulbs that Mathilde found too weak lit the mess room. Lannec put his elbows on the table and leaned over his steaming bowl of coffee for the ten minutes that he allowed himself after getting up.

A nor'wester while they were still over the Flanders Banks meant they would have a foul night, possibly with mist into the bargain. It would soon be time to think about that.

A newspaper that had been used to wrap something was lying on the green baize, and Lannec pulled it over, without thinking and without meaning to read it. It was a local paper from a Seine estuary town, open at the classified advertisements page.

Brasserie-Restaurant Chandivert
The most modern and the most fun
Live music every day

Lannec looked at his wife's cabin door and then at a porthole streaked with rain that was getting ever heavier.

Caen . . . The Brasserie Chandivert . . . Rain . . . Mathilde . . . Their engagement.

Rain, especially, and particularly evening rain . . . He went into Chandivert's one rainy evening when he was skipper of a boat that was unloading at Caen.

Ghostly figures swept along the ill-lit pavement, but the huge brasserie was warm and lively, full of laughter and talk, with music playing, billiard balls clicking and glasses clinking. It smelled of beer, coffee and grilled sausage.

To be honest, Lannec was looking to pick up a woman when he saw Mathilde sitting there with her mother. He even remembered they appeared to be eating their cake at a snail's pace so as to enjoy it for as long they could.

Why did he play around making eyes at the girl? She smiled. Then he laughed. Her mother didn't get what was going on and looked at the other tables.

'Go to the toilets,' Lannec's eyes said.

He was wearing his best captain's uniform and had just had a shave. In the end the girl got up and went to the toilets, where he caught up with her.

'Can't I ever see you on your own?'

She was so taken aback by his boldness that she burst out in a nervous laugh.

'Won't you answer me?'

'I don't know you . . .'

'Well, I'll find out who you are! I'll find out where you live and wait for you at the door.'

He didn't really believe he would, but all the same, out of idleness and just for fun, he followed them to an address in Rue Saint-Pierre, where they lived over a shoe shop.

'Campois!'

The steward emerged from his store room, where he sat like a spider in the middle of its web.

'Is my wife asleep?'

'I don't know, sir.'

Lannec drank a sip of coffee and lit the pipe he'd just filled. Some memories, even if they were stupid ones, made him sentimental: long waits in a dark street in the evening, Mathilde turning up to say she could not go out with him, or a letter she threw to him from a window that he had to pick up out of the mud.

He downed the remainder of the coffee, sighed, stood up, took his oilskins off the hook and wrapped his neck in his blue wool scarf. Just before leaving the mess room he glanced at the cabin door, and it opened.

'Émile!' his wife called out.

'Yes.'

'I want to inform you of one thing: I shan't set foot in the mess room again unless we eat together alone.'

'But . . .'

'The others can easily have their dinners separately.'

Upon which, she shut the door. Lannec slowly went up the staircase, and once he got to the deck he scowled on seeing the way the sea was getting heavier. Two men ran past in the dark and he grabbed one of them – the bos'n.

'What is it?'

'We're tying down the cows. One of them almost broke a leg already.'

The *Tonnerre-de-Dieu* was a good ship, no doubt about that. But like all old English vessels she was long and narrow, which made her roll a great deal.

Lannec got to the bridge and saw the shape of Georges Moinard and behind him that of Monsieur Gilles. He said hallo in his usual way, with a grunt. Then he looked out for the lighthouses in range, glanced at the compass and, if need be, at the chart.

'South Foreland?' he queried as he pointed through the drizzle to an intermittent light.

In making that suggestion he was taking the upwind into account, because with the following current they should have been much further on.

'I think it's Dover,' Moinard replied with furrowed brow.

If it was Dover, then they had so to speak been standing still since two o'clock.

'Aren't you sure it's Dover?'

'Look! There are two lights . . .'

For the last fifteen minutes the first mate and Monsieur Gilles had both been watching those two on-and-off lights where there should have been only one.

'Must be a ship's light, for sure.'

'Yes, but which one is it?'

The three of them spent the next ten minutes staring at the same point in the sea until the lights separated sufficiently to enable them to be identified.

'Wheel to starboard!' Lannec ordered. 'About time, too!'

With the wind now athwart, the ship started rolling as if in a real storm, and the cattle were soaked in spray. For a moment Lannec's mind turned to his wife in her cabin, no doubt lying down and waiting for each successive roll and yaw.

'What's that ahead of us?'

'A fishing boat, I think. Those men never light their mast-head lanterns.'

'By the way, Moinard . . . I've got to tell you something . . . about my wife.'

He spat and shook out his pipe.

'She's asked to take her meals separately, with me. If it doesn't bother you, you'll have a sitting together with the other officers after we've had our meal.'

'It doesn't bother me.'

He was lying. It bothered both men equally. It was so inappropriate that it even made them feel embarrassed for the ship.

'You know something? I don't think she'll come with us again . . .'

'It's up to her.'

That was the way Moinard was. He took things as they came without trying to change the course of events, unlike Lannec, who was up in arms over the slightest change.

'It's getting thicker!'

Rain had turned to drizzle, and the drizzle was now gradually turning into a fog that put a ring of haze around the lighthouse and made it seem further away.

'Gilles! Sound the siren!'

The three of them were very calm, just a bit more grumpy than usual, because they'd have to spend the night on lookout, trying to distinguish the lighthouse beams through the fog and having their eardrums pummelled by the fog horn.

The radio operator came up for a turn on the bridge and after only a few minutes without saying anything he let drop as if it were a matter of no consequence:

'It's really bad further up. There's a boat off Ijmuiden that's already asking for radio assistance to find her course.'

Lannec didn't know why, but he looked at the man askance. What was happening wasn't unusual. It was just seasonal weather. He'd done this trip a hundred times in far worse conditions, when visibility was so near to nil that you had to listen out for the sound of waves breaking to guess where the sandbanks were.

He rang for Campois and spoke to him from the top of the bridge ladder.

'You'll serve dinner for me and my wife, then do a second sitting for the officers.'

Two hours went by.

'Aren't you going to take a break?' Lannec asked Moinard.

He knew very well that he wouldn't. Two men were better than one, and three were better than two at finding the lights in this filthy fog. Lannec took the bearings of the South Foreland light every thirty minutes. When he'd done the calculations in the chart room, Moinard looked at him inquiringly.

'Barely more than three knots!' the captain answered.

They had not just the wind but the tide against them. The steersman had to reset the course of the *Tonnerre-de-Dieu* at every lurch, as the sea was constantly pushing her in the wrong direction.

'My wife can't be enjoying this!'

He said it out of revenge, but he didn't really mean it, or rather, he took no pleasure in imagining Mathilde writhing with seasickness.

When the dinner bell rang, he turned to Moinard.

'I'll be back up in ten minutes. If there's any need . . .'

He could have wept in fury at the idea that on his own boat, and on its first voyage to boot, every tradition of the merchant navy was being thrown overboard. He therefore put on his most ponderous gait and his harshest face as he entered the mess room, shook out his oilskins and hung it up on its hook.

'My wife isn't . . .'

He hadn't got past the start of his sentence before Mathilde came out of her cabin and took her place at table as straightfor-wardly as she would have in their dining room in Caen. She was wearing a modest black silk dress and had combed her hair, powdered her face and put on a touch of lipstick.

'Aren't you seasick?'

'What do you care?'

He took his napkin from its ring and unfolded it without a word while Campois served the soup. He was lost, suspended between feelings of humiliation and fury. He felt as if the entire crew were laughing at him and looking down on him with disapproval.

He had had to inform the chief engineer, the radio operator and everyone . . . that madame wished to take her meals alone with monsieur!

Mathilde looked a bit pale but she ate nonetheless. Yet the sea was so heavy that they had had to set up the side boards to stop plates sliding off the table.

'Not even a bit queasy?'

'I've told you, no.'

Lannec suspected there was a smile in Campois' blue eyes, and that made him even angrier.

'There's never been anything like this,' he grunted after noisily slurping down his soup and pushing away his empty plate.

'There's nothing wrong with a new start.'

He was powerless. It felt out of kilter, almost indecent. He felt ridiculous sitting on his own with his wife while his officers, and especially Moinard, waited to eat after them, like servants!

In his eyes, it undermined the order and harmony of the whole boat and crew.

'Why ever did you think of coming along?'

He wasn't yet saying it, but the answer was in his mind: *'Because your mother wanted you to keep an eye on her money, didn't she?'*

He hated Dame Pitard, as he called her, along with all the lady aunts and cousins who bore the same name.

'A fat lot of good it's done you!'

'So you have a better time when you leave me behind?'

She said that just as Campois was serving the vegetables. Lannec waited for him to leave the room, put his fork down and looked his wife in the eye.

'What are you insinuating?'

'Do you imagine Marcel doesn't take advantage of your being away?'

She didn't need to look at Lannec to know that his face had turned crimson. For above Dame Pitard and the lady aunts, Lannec hated one person even more, a man with a name whose very syllables caused the captain to boil with rage.

Marcel! She hadn't wasted any time! The second time he'd seen Mathilde, in Caen, in the street, she'd made sure to ask him:

'Do you know Marcel?'

'Marcel who?'

She uttered the name like Jesus Christ or Napoleon, as if the whole world knew who Marcel was.

'The violinist.'

'What violinist?'

'At Chandivert's.'

He had seen plenty of Marcel since then, because during their engagement he'd had to go to Chandivert's with Dame Pitard almost every evening to listen to the music.

Mathilde always managed to get seats near the rostrum, and there was always a flush on her cheeks. She would whisper to Lannec:

'Can't you see how passionate he is?'

But the fiancé was more furious still at the way she was constantly fussing about that sickly young man with wavy hair who made eyes at her as he plied his bow.

'If he tries anything, I'll smash his face in, I will!'

'You're being beastly. He can't help being in love with me, can he?'

To top it all, Marcel made eyes exactly the same way at every little miss in his audience.

It was even worse when, aboard his own boat, at sea, she started talking about that Marcel!

'Say that again!' he said, slowly.

'Do you imagine Marcel doesn't take advantage . . .'

'To do what, precisely?'

'To pursue me.'

'Nothing else?'

'A woman without a husband for weeks on end . . .'

'And that's all?'

'Why should he stop there? Do you stop short when you're in Antwerp or Hamburg or wherever and collect photos of girls you leave in your jacket pocket?'

'That's something else. I'm talking about Marcel . . .'

Lannec was all the more furious because he knew Campois was in his cubbyhole in the gangway and could hear every word.

'Marcel came round to comfort me. You're the one who's asking, right? You're the one who's blaming me for coming on the trip . . .'

'Have you got the cheek to claim that . . .'

'Yes!'

'. . . that the two of you . . . ?'

'Yes, we did, and so there! And if you really want to know, I can tell you we'd done it before I ever met you! Serves you right, so . . .'

She didn't finish her sentence. Lannec got up and brought the flat of his big hand down on her cheek so hard that Mathilde's head hit the back of the bench seat.

He was aware of the impact, of the pain he'd caused, and of Campois' fright, but he strode to the door taking no notice of the steward with his back to the bulkhead and went out on deck.

'Campois! Bring me my oilskins and sou'wester!'

The rain calmed him down. He was breathing noisily. He ran his hands through his hair three or four times, and when he'd put on his wet-weather clothes he climbed up the bridge ladder.

'Is it clearing?'

The siren wasn't being sounded because visibility had improved a little. You could see two or three lights on the English coast, to port, and to starboard there was the Walde light, near Calais.

Fifteen minutes' silence ensued as he wandered between Moinard and Monsieur Gilles, until at last the dinner bell rang.

'You can both go down now!'

Once again he was on his own alongside the steersman standing stock still at the wheel. As a diversion from his fury he plotted his position twice over, quite pointlessly, because he knew these waters very well. Then he set the wheel left hand down a bit to make sure the boat was on the roughest course possible.

Hopefully that would make Mathilde seasick at last!

When the officers came back up half an hour later they found Lannec at his post with his forehead close up to the mist-covered window.

'There's trouble ahead, Moinard.'

The first mate looked at him with an expression of surprise.

'Oh, not the boat,' he added. 'I mean trouble with the wife.'

By eleven o'clock the wind was even stronger. The *Tonnerre-de-Dieu* lurched from one wall of water to another and, each time, she shuddered from stem to stern. They had had to slow down the engine, because the boat wasn't fully loaded, and every heavy pitch brought the screw above the waterline and had it turning wildly in the air.

At least the fog had gone, but there was water running over everything – the deck, the bulkheads, faces, oilskins. There was even water in Lannec's tobacco and pipe, which kept on going out.

Moinard had gone to sleep ahead of taking his watch at midnight. Monsieur Gilles had nothing much to do and shuttled back and forth between the bridge and the telegraph room, bringing news.

'Paul's talking to the ship you can see to starboard, a Dutchman returning from the Black Sea. The first mate is a friend of his . . .'

You could hear the dynamo whirring. The one-eyed radio operator sat quite still in his cluttered cabin with headphones on his ears and his finger on the switch.

'Boulogne harbourmaster requests all shipping to report sighting of a fishing vessel out of contact that should have docked at twelve hundred . . .'

Could it be the one they'd seen without its mast light in late afternoon?

'Tell Paul to report it just in case, and give them our position at eighteen hundred.'

Lannec drank a glass of spirits and offered one to his first mate. As they stood there with glasses in their hands, the skipper thought the young man was staring at him inquisitively.

'What are you looking at?'

'Me? Nothing . . .'

'So I've been cheated on. There's nothing so special about that!'

He threw his empty glass into the sea, leaned on the railing and scowled. He'd completely forgotten the business about the ghost, but just then a man wrapped in a bed sheet moved past on the gangway below, between the forecastle deck and the store room.

The man looked up, saw the skipper and winked at him, as if to say, 'You see, I'm obeying your order!'

It was the bos'n going to put the ham back.

Lannec glanced at the Calais light and then looked down, as he was curious to see how Campois would react.

What came from the store room was a scream, a scream so horrendous that it made one of the cows stand up with a start and snap its tether. A white shape reappeared on deck, but you couldn't see it as a human shape. Something was struggling wildly beneath the white sheet and trying to break free.

'Go and see what's going on,' Lannec said to Monsieur Gilles.

One of the crew came running to see to the cow that was charging round the deck and making the steel plates thunder.

The steersman was the only one to stay quite still, though he glanced at the captain now and again as if to ask him what was up.

'Call Moinard!' Monsieur Gilles could be heard shouting. 'He must have the key to the medicine cabinet.'

Lannec lost sight of the to-do as the white shape vanished

inside. He could just hear people walking, doors opening and closing and a continuous wail in lieu of the original scream of pain.

He was champing at the bit. He couldn't leave his watch, and there was nobody to keep him in the picture.

He shuddered all of a sudden. There was a man standing stock still beside him with a mournful air. It was Campois, who had never put on quite such a tragic face as he did now.

'What are you doing here?'

'I am handing myself in.'

'Eh? Did you kill the bos'n, or what?'

The steward shook his head and clasped his hands together like a vice.

'Speak up! What did you do?'

Campois gulped down his saliva between every word.

'I expected the ghost to return . . .'

In that state the steward looked more like a village idiot than a normal human being.

'You shot it?'

'I didn't have a gun.'

'Well, then! Say something, *tonnerre de Dieu!*'

'I balanced a pot of boiling water on the top edge of the door. I don't mind if I go to prison!'

His eyes were shining. Perhaps he was glad to be free of a great weight at long last. He'd stopped believing in ghosts a few moments earlier.

'Go to your bunk.'

'Will I go to prison?'

'Go to bed.'

Groans could still be heard, but they weren't continuous, which meant that Moinard, who had a medical certificate, was giving the bos'n first aid.

'Gilles!' Lannec shouted.

He came up in a few minutes later with an expression on his face that was half tragic and half amused.

'Well?'

'The bos'n's face looks like a tomato. He got a whole bucket of hot water over his head. Fortunately the water had been standing for a few minutes and had gone off the boil. The only thing is, Campois used the biggest of the copper pots, and it slashed the bos'n's forehead.'

'Is it serious?'

'Moinard told the bos'n with a straight face that if he carried on writhing and screaming, he would have to unpeel his scalp. That kept the man quiet, but he's rolling his eyes something dreadful . . .'

'Captain!' someone said shyly.

Lannec turned round and saw the steersman, who was stock still as usual, jutting his chin towards the stem and, a few cable-lengths out, a green light and a red light that had just come into sight.

'Hard to port!'

A few seconds later an English liner bound for India passed so close to the *Tonnerre-de-Dieu* you could make out the passengers' faces through the portholes of the first-class smoking lounge.

4.

Lannec would go up to Moinard pretending to be thinking about something else, but with a malicious look in his eye. He would cough, fill his pipe or look at the sea as if it would tell him something, then blurt out in a mumble:

'Georges, you know, you mustn't let it get you down. I'll get rid of her in Hamburg . . .'

That usually happened on the bridge, but if Lannec saw the chief engineer checking a capstan then he'd feel the need to go down on deck with hands in pockets and a distracted or innocent look on his face.

'She must be having a dreadful bout of seasickness, don't you think!?'

The sea was still heavy, the weather still grey and cold, with calmer spells always followed by squalls of rain. When they passed near sandbanks – and there were many of them on the course they had set – the angry undertow tossed the *Tonnerre-de-Dieu* around and made its seams rattle.

The cows had stopped moving for the last forty-eight hours, and they'd stopped eating as well. When they raised their muzzles it wasn't to graze, but to let rivulets of glutinous snot drip to the ground.

The bos'n, now wrapped in bandages that made his head the size of a diver's helmet, fed them with coffee beans and then pepper seeds, but to no effect. The animals watched him come up to them with dull eyes that had lost all hope.

'Well, Georges, what would you do if you were in my shoes?'

Lannec could go for an hour or even two without speaking about it, but then it got the better of him. He'd even talked about it with the bos'n, saying with glee:

'The old girl must be taking a real thrashing!'

The men didn't really respond. They looked away. Or muttered something incomprehensible.

Moinard was married and had three children; the eldest had just finished secondary school. The chief engineer was a widower, and the bos'n's wife ran a grocery somewhere in Normandy.

There was one man Lannec did not speak to about it: the one-eyed radio operator, who for his part kept his distance as if the captain's behaviour revolted him.

But Lannec hadn't done anything! He had settled on not dining with Mathilde, who had her meal served half an hour before the men. As she spent the rest of the time in her cabin, he hadn't seen her for two days – since he'd slapped her, to be precise.

But she was on his mind far more than he would have liked. When he went below, for instance, he always looked into the galley and he could tell from the washing-up whether or not Mathilde had eaten anything.

'Isn't she vomiting?' he asked Campois.

'Couldn't say either way. I reckon she's too proud to let it be seen.'

Like her mother, *tonnerre de Dieu*! Women who don't look the part, but are as strong-willed, or I should say stubborn, as mules!

Lannec had gone back to his usual routine. At sea, he didn't shave, he barely washed and he let his braces hang loose until noon. He was having his meals with the other officers now, and since he knew that Mathilde could hear everything going on in the mess room from her cabin, he made a point of being loud and jolly.

'OK, men! Can't wait to get to Hamburg and have some fun! I know a few dives in the city, and there's a gorgeous blonde . . .'

As he spoke he glared at the closed cabin door and then at his shipmates, who stifled their grins.

'You'll come along with me, Moinard, won't you?'

Moinard gave a non-committal shrug. Everyone on board knew very well that Moinard never took shore leave. He'd got it into his head to study Einstein's theories and had acquired a shelfful of books about relativity, which he pored over with great intensity.

'You don't understand a word of it!' Lannec often told him.

That might well have been true, but Moinard had resolved to understand some if it one day.

Lannec ate noisily and, glancing once again at the door, came out with:

'You see, women are good for you-know-what. But for anything else, you should pay no more attention to them than to an old tea-chest bobbing in the sea.'

He took twice as many watches as was useful. He sent Moinard off to rest or to learn mathematics and spent hours on the bridge, where the steersman heard him talking to himself.

'Another good gale in the offing!' he would declare on inspecting the sky.

He was thinking of Mathilde, who must have been pale and vomiting in her cabin. It just wasn't possible she could take it. A minute later, in fact, he would call the steward.

'Isn't she vomiting?'

'She hasn't called.'

She was too proud! And if she had lied to him, she was too proud to admit it!

They had lost more than a day struggling against the upwind

but even so they were approaching the Outer Elbe. They raised the signal flag to summon the Cuxhaven pilot.

It was morning. Night had not quite faded from the sky and you could see the streetlamps on shore still lit up. Thin, cold rain was falling when a motor launch came alongside and a pilot in a green uniform hauled himself up to the deck. When he got to the bridge he gave a military salute.

Two or three lines of ships clustered like ants between the buoys marking the passage to Hamburg, and all around there was a throbbing of diesel engines and the soot and vapour of steam-powered boats.

'Take a drink to the Fritz!' Lannec told the steward as he went down to his cabin.

It was a ritual. Whenever they came into port and took on a pilot, Lannec left Moinard in charge and went to have a good scrub like workmen do on Sunday mornings. His cabin suddenly smelled of soap, eau de cologne and shaving cream. Campois never forgot to lay out on the skipper's bunk a starched shirt, a stiff collar, detachable cuffs and Lannec's newest suit – a civilian suit with grey-striped trousers.

Lannec carried on muttering half-sentences to himself as he changed, and when he was all done, in shoes that creaked, with dabs of talcum powder behind his ears and brilliantine in his hair, he sat down in the mess room and pulled over the blotter.

'*Go back home and say hi to Marcel from me,*' he wrote first off.

He squinted at the door, then at the factory chimneys he could see through a porthole, then screwed up the paper and took another sheet.

'*Go back home . . .*'

He was on the point of getting up and calling out to his wife to say . . . To say what?

'*Go back home . . .*'

That was all that was needed. He slipped the note into an

envelope, took 2,000 francs out of a steel safe that held the ship's treasury and called Campois.

'Give that to my wife.'

'What time do I go to jail?'

He wouldn't let up on his idea. It had become an obsession.

'We'll see when we get back to France. Hand me my over-coat and gloves.'

When he got to the bridge all prepared to go into town, the *Tonnerre-de-Dieu* was already at the mouth of the Altona dock. A launch approached and came alongside with a buzzing noise, and a moment later a short, bald man climbed up on deck with some difficulty and leaned down to grab hold of the leather briefcase that a sailor handed up to him.

The pilot stood stock still with his left hand on the wheel and his right hand nursing a glass of spirits that he was slowly warming up. The engine was on dead slow. Other ships were moving all around them, some under their own steam, others hauled by tugs, but above all there were hundreds of small boats, launches and service boats in a jam as dense as traffic on a city street.

In the background, on the deserted quayside, you could see a tram that still had its lights on, presumably a workmen's tram, and thousands of houses still in the dark.

The fat, bald man was the shipping agent, who worked with Bernheim, in Rouen. First he spoke to the pilot in German and told him which basin they had been assigned.

'The rail wagons are ready and waiting, and we'll start unloading in an hour,' he told Lannec. 'We were expecting you yesterday.'

They went into the chart house, where Lannec stood a round of drinks and got out his customs clearance, which he handed to the agent.

'No passengers?'

'My wife.'

One, two then three launches surrounded the *Tonnerre-de-Dieu* as it moved slowly into the mooring that had been assigned. Harbour police came on board and up to the bridge, then came the customs officers and two ship's chandlers, who started talking right away to the bos'n to find out what new stores were needed on board.

Lannec felt good. His shoes squeaked. He'd got out the traditional cigar box and as he chatted he wondered if Mathilde had already read his note.

What he wanted above all was to avoid seeing her! She should not try to talk to him! In any case, to ward off such a possibility, he was going to go ashore right away.

'By the way, Moinard, I'm going to the consulate first, then to the shipbroker, all over the place! I may not be back on board before evening. If my wife leaves . . .'

Moinard gave him a serious look.

'Don't stop her! And also, get the bos'n to have his wound dressed by a doctor . . .'

While the dockhands were still pulling in the hawsers, Lannec went down into a small boat, which two seamen manoeuvred to shore. It was dirty and greasy. Lannec stayed standing so as not to soil his clothes, and he had a hard time getting up the iron ladder without smudging himself.

The city hadn't yet come alive. All the cranes were at work, but nothing else. Lannec had to keep his eyes on the ground to avoid puddles and rails, and also ahead of him, because skips were swinging over him at little more than head-height.

Wearing a pearl-grey hat, he wove his way between rail wagons and horses. He walked past stacks of chests that smelled of cinnamon, so he reckoned he was next to an ocean-going vessel that had come in from the Far East.

He knew the way to go. In fact, it was pretty much the only thing he knew in most of the ports he put in to: the route that went to the harbourmaster's office, from there to the customs office, and on to the French consulate.

Like the shipping agent, he had a briefcase under his arm, but his was made of fine yellow leather.

He had to wait for the harbourmaster, but in the end he got into the office and had the ship's log book stamped. It was nine o'clock when he stepped through the iron railings that separate the world of the sea from the world of land.

There was something else he knew: the number of the tram he had to catch. He waited a few minutes for it to come, stepped up on to the platform at the back and got off in a quiet street with wet cobblestones, right opposite the French consulate.

When he'd talked in the mess room about knowing low dives in Hamburg, he'd been lying, just to annoy his wife. It's true he'd caught sight of the red-light district from afar once or twice, but he'd never set foot inside it.

He didn't know any of the street names, either. He had his own bearings: the Paris railway station, the Berlin railway station, the Grand Theatre and Sankt Nikolai's Church.

He sometimes took a wrong turn but soon realized it and always got to his destination in the end without having to ask for directions.

When he came out of the consulate at 10.30, he went into a *Stube* and had sausages and potato salad. He always ate at the same place when he was in Hamburg; the owner knew him by sight.

'Are you still with the *Agen*?'

'No. I've got my own ship now, the *Tonnerre-de-Dieu*.'

'*Ach so!*'

He wasn't hungry but he ate the sausages because it was a tradition to eat sausages at that time of day on each of his port calls. Then he caught a taxi to the agent's office, because he hadn't been there before.

All shipping agents have the same office, the same counter, the same back lounge and the same bottle of whisky. Lannec encountered the same plump and bald fellow he'd seen in the morning.

'Well?'

'You'll have finished unloading in an hour. There was an extra crane and a crew available, so I put them on the job as well. As for Madame Lannec . . .'

Lannec looked up sharply.

'I mentioned her to the police. They wanted to see her to ask for her passport . . .'

'Well, it's perfectly valid . . .'

'Yes, it is. Madame Lannec showed it to them. But she declared she didn't intend to come ashore. As for your bos'n, he's with a French doctor this very moment.'

All shipping agents have a comfortable armchair for smoking a cigar and drinking whisky while talking business.

'In addition, I've got an offer to make. Are you in a hurry to get back to France?'

'Tell me what you've got.'

'A big load of railway equipment to deliver to Iceland. About a thousand tons! It's a big rush, and we first thought of a motor-powered sailboat, but the captain said no because he had a wooden hull . . .'

'Hang on. What did my wife tell you?'

'Not me, skipper. She told the police! She said she had no reason to go ashore. As for the freight, they are offering . . .'

Lannec downed his whisky in one gulp and cast a longing glance at the maritime chart on the wall showing the vast expanse of stormy sea between Hamburg and Iceland. He could have marked all the places where at that time of year the waves rise up like sheer walls to eight or even ten metres in height.

'As it's a rush job, they're not going to quibble about pfennigs per ton . . .'

Lannec stood up and served himself a second glass of whisky. 'I'll take it!' he said.

Big pieces of steel make an awkward cargo, because if they're not well stowed they can make a hole in the hull as soon as the ship rolls. And it was a lousy course to set in November, especially in a boat as narrow as the *Tonnerre-de-Dieu*.

But so what!

'When do we load?'

'This afternoon. I'll bring the charter party to the boat. The lading will be completed by tomorrow evening.'

He went and had another pint in a bar near the station and finally got back to the familiar surroundings of the harbour. He'd got mud on his shoes, and his hat was wet. The cranes were just finishing the unloading as he went back on board, and the bos'n was back from the doctor and giving Moinard his medical certificate.

Lannec went straight down to the mess room.

'Campois!'

The sad, scared face of the steward appeared.

'What did she say?' the captain whispered as he pointed at the closed cabin door.

Campois took a yellow envelope from under the green baize on the table, where he had hidden it. The message said: '*I am not leaving. The ship is mine as much as yours.*'

That was Mathilde's reply, and in a fit of anger Lannec slammed his two fists into the cabin door.

'Mathilde! Mathilde! I need to talk to you . . .'

Scuffling noises from inside, then the door opened a slit, and a calm figure with a wan face appeared.

'We're taking on freight for Iceland!'

'So what?'

'You can't come along with us.'

'We'll see about that.'

'But *tonnerre de Dieu*, what the . . .'

The door slammed shut, and Lannec had no choice but to go and talk to Moinard.

'Georges, old chap, we've been offered a golden opportunity: rail wagons in parts for Reykjavik.'

Moinard looked at the smoke-grey sky and the sea that even in the harbour was tossing around like water boiling in a pot.

'What do you say?'

'And your wife?'

'Now do you think I'm going to turn down a bargain just because one of those Pitards . . .'

He thumped his hand on the desk in the chart house before reaching the conclusion:

'We're taking it, *tonnerre de Dieu*! And that's her hard luck! As if women were allowed to steer the boat . . .'

Half an hour later he was in his cabin, wiping the mud off his shoes and giving a good brush to his trouser cuffs.

'Gilles!' he called as the second mate came into the mess room. 'How about a night on the town?'

'If you like.'

They went ashore together, leaving Moinard to oversee the loading of the freight.

'I know a restaurant, over here . . .'

They got lost and spent half an hour finding the restaurant, where they got a table next to the window.

It was here that more than six years ago Lannec had once picked up a short, dark woman as hard as a hazelnut and taken her to the cinema. That's why he looked at all the women in the place, but they were already taken or paid no attention to the two sailors.

'Paul's in love, isn't he? Of course he is! You can tell me! Whether it's Marcel or Paul, what difference does it make?'

He was overexcited. He was talking loudly and ordered three bottles of Rhine wine one after the other.

At three o'clock they went for a walk under the colonnade of the Central Station, which with its two rows of shops is always packed with people.

'How about that one? A pity she's on her own . . .'

They needed two women, and half a dozen times they followed pairs of women only to turn around after a while on realizing they weren't interested.

All the same, that was where on another occasion, last year . . .

'There won't be any fun in Reykjavik! And I can think of someone who's going to be as sick as a dog on the way there. But tell me, do have you a clue what she's after?'

They'd already downed three or four glasses of spirits, and Lannec was talking to Monsieur Gilles as a chum. The second mate's head was buzzing, and his eyes were glazed.

'No, I don't.'

'And nor do I, *tonnerre de Dieu*! If only she would admit she lied to me! But it wasn't a lie! I know that Marcel, and I should have guessed there was something going on . . . Look over there! . . .'

Two women were passing by and dawdling in front of shop windows. The men took up position behind them. They smiled, and the girls smiled back.

Lannec knew only twenty words of German, but he was fluent in English.

The two couples sauntered from shop window to shop window and finally went into a cinema together.

One of the women was tall and sturdy, with a nice face and a kindly, ironical smile. Lannec chose her. The other woman was shorter and slimmer, with a small, pointed bosom. She couldn't keep still and kept on teasing Monsieur Gilles, who smiled awkwardly.

They had yet another drink at the cinema bar. Then they

went to have an aperitif in a restaurant with live music, just like Chandivert's.

Lannec was flushed with excitement. He chattered away in a mixture of French and English with his few German words thrown in, whereas his partner, Anna, answered in English.

For dinner, the girls took the two men to a kind of bistro in Sankt-Pauli, and Monsieur Gilles spent half the time on the dance-floor with his new friend.

'Have you really got your own boat? Is it a big one?'

'Really big!'

'Why aren't you in a uniform?'

Now they were drinking sparkling wine, and Lannec was loudly explaining the difference between German champagne and the real stuff from France.

By midnight they were drunk. In a whisper, Monsieur Gilles begged his partner, who was called Else, to slip away with him discreetly. But she didn't want to part from her sister, because she claimed Anna really was her sister.

'All aboard! . . .' Lannec thundered. 'We'll show you what real champagne is like!'

The plan nearly came unstuck when the women took fright on seeing the dock area that had to be crossed. Monsieur Gilles carried his partner in his arms over the puddles and the mud and nearly fell over.

'Ahoy there, *Tonnerre-de-Dieu*!' Lannec shouted once they reached the plank that served as a gangway.

Campois emerged from the dark and threw a lantern over to him.

'Lend a hand to these ladies!'

They weren't at ease until they were on board and they only calmed down in the mess room, where the two men took their coats.

'Champagne!' Lannec ordered. 'And find that tin of caviar that must be there somewhere . . .'

He stared furiously at the cabin door.

'Come over here, sweetheart!'

He'd forgotten Anna didn't understand French. But he smacked a few noisy kisses on her cheeks, any old how, thinking that behind that door Mathilde would go pale on hearing what he was doing.

'Three bottles! Four bottles!' he yelled to Campois, who scurried around as if he were the one at fault.

Lannec was dreadfully tired but he clenched his teeth and cast his eyes over Anna with stern determination to find her attractive.

'Don't think of holding back, Monsieur Gilles! We're on our *own* ship now . . .'

His small eyes smiled, hardened and smiled again, then he felt like punching down the cabin door.

'Our *own* ship, *tonnerre de Dieu!*'

5.

He never needed to be woken up. Whatever the circumstances, Émile Lannec was up at six – and at five, or even four, in the summer. When he opened his eyes this time, he found the cabin light on and himself on his bunk still in his socks and trousers. As he stood up and made his way to the bathroom to slap water on his face, he saw a couple of images in his mind's eye and was pleased . . . Gentle Anna kissing him on the mouth in a strangely liquid way and stroking his chest through his open shirt . . . Monsieur Gilles tottering over to the opposite side of the mess room with the other girl . . .

He brushed his teeth energetically, rinsed out with mouthwash and to get rid of the lingering taste lit his first pipe of the day. When he opened the cabin door he was wearing carpet slippers without socks, had his trousers askew on his hips and had done up only half the buttons on his workday pea-jacket. It was still dark in the mess room. He stood still for a moment, listened to the sound of breathing and made out a face and a naked female foot.

He walked on with a shrug and went into the galley, where Campois was making filter coffee. He noticed empty champagne bottles and dirty glasses on the sideboard and gave a joyless wink to the steward.

'Give me my coffee.'

He drank it standing up, half in the galley and half on deck. It was a very cold day. The same workmen's trams were there as the day before. When daylight broke through the dark air he could make out black shapes scurrying along beside the factory walls and imagined red noses and chilly hands stuffed into coat pockets.

'Haven't they started the lading yet?' he asked Campois on seeing the gaping holds.

'Something came up, I don't know what, but they're only loading this morning.'

Still sleepy men trickled off the forecastle deck to fetch their mugs of coffee. Then there was a noise from below, and Moinard appeared, buttoning up his jacket. He gave his hand to the skipper as he did every morning and refrained from mentioning what had happened during the night. He simply said:

'We have to be at berth 27 by seven. There were some problems yesterday, but the agent told me that they've all been sorted out.'

'Good! Stand by to weigh anchor!' Lannec ordered.

He went down and found the mess room in a light as cloudy as the half-empty glasses cluttering the table. Monsieur Gilles had made up his bed on the bench seat and was sleeping with his mouth open and his hand trailing down to the floor. One of the women was using his overcoat as a pillow and the other, lying awkwardly, was beginning to open her eyes.

'Shake a leg!' Lannec grunted as he gave them a shove.

He wasn't even trying to speak German now. He'd also forgotten that the women understood English. His small eyes were hard, and in his work clothes he made such a brutal impression that the women barely recognized their partner of last night.

Anna wanted to go back to sleep. The other girl moaned and asked for a glass of water. Lannec poured it out for her and then pulled them both upright and handed them their clothes in a pile.

Monsieur Gilles sat up in his bunk and looked on the scene with alarm. Like all young men, he was slow to gather his wits.

The girls' dresses were crumpled, and their silk stockings were twisted halfway down their legs. One of Anna's suspenders was broken, and the girls' skin, especially their thighs, looked livid in the poor light.

Lannec popped into his cabin, came back with two 100-franc notes and gave one to each girl. They protested because they wanted marks, but Lannec paid no attention and hustled them to the stairway.

He lent an ear to the noise from the deck. The hawsers were being pulled in already. Less than six minutes after opening their eyes, Anna and Else, still damp from sleep, were back on the cold, grey quayside as the ship's anchor was winched up.

Lannec went back to the bridge to be with Moinard and took charge of the manoeuvre, but at one point he couldn't not glance at the two figures lingering on the quay, looking quite pathetic. He nudged his mate with his elbow and tried to smile.

He hadn't bothered to get to the bottom of what he remembered from the night before and began to wonder whether he'd made love to Anna or not.

'So where is it then, this berth 27?'

No! As far as he was concerned things couldn't have gone that far. As for Monsieur Gilles . . .

'Dead slow ahead!'

It was a difficult manoeuvre in such a crowded harbour, and Lannec, with the stem of his pipe firmly clamped between his teeth, made it a point of honour to complete it in the least possible time, without any hesitation but not without giving his mate a fright.

Berth 27 came into sight, with wagon wheels, axles and bogeys piled up on the dock, but there seemed scarcely enough room for the *Tonnerre-de-Dieu* between two Baltic clippers – small ships of 400 tons – that were already tied up.

'There's something funny going on,' Lannec muttered as he leaned over and put the engines in reverse.

He could smell it. He saw five men on the quayside watching the *Tonnerre-de-Dieu* dock. The shipping agent emerged from the group, came up to the water's edge, cupped his hands to his mouth and shouted out something Lannec could not understand.

'Do we stick with it?'

The shore group included the masters of the two clippers, who must have been the ones in yellow clogs. The whole thing looked like a conspiracy. Lannec grasped that at first glance.

'Just you wait and see!' he grunted.

He scared the lot of them. He moved abreast the first clipper, almost shaving its side, then abruptly went astern, slipped straight in to the gap and brought the *Tonnerre-de-Dieu* to a halt at the berth within an inch of crushing the bowsprit of the other boat.

The proof that something unhealthy was afoot was that nobody moved a limb to secure the hawsers until the shipping agent himself took it on. He came on board straight away, waving his arms, in quite a state, and explained in his poor French that the load to Iceland was off the books.

His eyes were puffy and his pupils narrow, but Lannec, who listened to the agent without responding, scanned and rescanned the competitors on shore who seemed to be challenging him.

What was going on was this: the Icelanders who had ordered the railway equipment had specified in the charge sheet that delivery had to be made in the shortest time available, but that, price for price, preference should be given to Danish-flagged vessels, since Iceland belonged to Denmark.

The previous day the Danish consul had learned that the Iceland mail boat would be leaving Copenhagen in five days' time and would take only six days to do the trip to Reykjavik.

Two clippers had undertaken to get the freight to Copenhagen in time for trans-shipment.

'Give me five minutes!' Lannec said to the agent.

It did him good to have an obstacle to overcome. In five minutes he was ready: not in a suit fit for a commercial traveller or a bank clerk, as he had been last night, but in heavy blue twill, with his captain's cap on his head and stubble on his cheeks.

By ten in the morning Moinard had still not heard from him. The stevedores cooled their heels on the dockside, and the clipper captains paced up and down, glancing now and again at the French tramp with fury in their eyes.

At 10.30 a taxi drew up. Lannec bounded out of it and went up to the agent, who was in more of a state than ever.

'Load up!' he yelled even before he got on board.

Game over! He'd won the match. He'd crisscrossed Hamburg from one consul to another and called Copenhagen on the telephone and he was still chomping on a fat cigar he'd been given somewhere or other.

The cranes screeched into action at his signal, and a first carriage chassis with its wheels attached swung through the air and over the hold.

On the other hand, when he got to the bridge he gave Moinard an odd look, and before saying anything, he poured himself a drink, coughed, filled his pipe and fiddled with things that were lying around. He was playing for time.

'Um, by the way, Georges . . .'

As usual, the self-effacing tone that Lannec put on and his shifty eyes meant that he'd done something stupid, or at least unwise.

'Do you know what I did to win?'

As each steel part settled into the hold, the whole ship shuddered, and it seemed the plates of the hull might come apart.

'Four days to Copenhagen and six days on the ocean-going mail boat made a ten-day trip, plus the cost of trans-shipment.

On the charter party I guaranteed we would do it in ten days, with a penalty for each day late.'

He looked down on the two small clippers with crushing scorn.

'It won't be easy!' he grunted as he went into the chart house and spread out the maps of the North Atlantic.

He plotted his course, roughly, measured the distances with his protractor and did the sums on a scrap of paper.

'Almost eighteen hundred sea miles! We make eight knots. Just enough margin to cope with one gale, but not two. But I have to go out again now. Seems our hawsers aren't strong enough to hold down the heavy pieces in the hold . . .'

He was back in two hours in a van with new steel cables and hawsers.

It wasn't raining but it was still cold and the roofs of the houses stuck up in the white air like shards of ice.

Lannec hadn't asked a single question about his wife all morning. But when he went down to the mess room between errands, he stopped for a few minutes, as if waiting for something. On his third visit, around five in the afternoon, he found Mathilde sitting at the green baize, writing a letter. Before he could open his mouth she got up, picked up her paper and penholder and went back into her cabin without a word.

'Mathilde!' he called shyly.

She didn't answer. He shrugged, feeling out of sorts and angry – with her, but also with himself.

He'd only seen her for a second, but he thought she had lost weight, got paler, and had bags under her eyes. There was a bitter look to her lips.

He remembered the slap. It was more than a slap! He'd hit her with all the strength of his heavy hand and he'd never forget the sound of bruised flesh that it made. What must it be like to be on the receiving end of a wallop like that, to feel defenceless and perhaps expecting more of the same?

He looked at the blotter in the vague hope of being able to read something on it. Was his wife writing to her mother, or to Marcel?

'Mathilde!'

He said that softly. He didn't want to be overheard by Campois.

'The blazes!' was all that came back from behind the door.

He took off his jacket and went down to the hold so as to supervise the stowage of the freight. North of the Scottish coast, thirty-foot waves aren't uncommon. In seas of that kind, it would be catastrophic if one of the big items came loose and started waltzing around down below.

Portable arc lights had been switched on so as to get a better view in the hold. Lannec rolled up his sleeves, strode over the axles, lifted steel wheels and secured the cables with his own hands. Now and again he pushed men aside who weren't working as fast as he wanted and did the job for them, showing his muscular torso and bulging arms.

But that didn't stop him thinking about other things, and suddenly he could be heard yelling:

'Call the radio man!'

Shortly after, the flabby head and single eye of Paul Lenglois could be seen leaning over the batten.

'Come down here!' Lannec ordered.

The only way down was a stepladder, and Lenglois was a clumsy man. An emotional weakling, he always managed to hurt himself performing even the easiest task.

Down in the hold, with the huge crane hook swinging over his head, Lannec looked Lenglois in the eye.

'You're going to go to my wife . . .'

The radio operator blushed, and Lannec went on:

'Don't be stupid. She's certainly aware you fancy her. You're forgetting she's cheated on me already . . .'

'She won't open her door for me,' Lenglois blurted out.

'Have you tried?'

He was sure he'd hit the nail on the head. Paul must have hung around her cabin door, definitely not with evil intent, but simply to comfort the young woman.

'She didn't open up?'

'She was crying . . . I asked her through the door if there was anything I could get for her . . .'

'Well then, try again. Insist. And when you do get in to see her, tell her, on your own behalf, that she simply cannot come along with us. Have you done the Iceland run before?'

'On a trawler.'

'So you know what it's like. We're going to have enough to worry about without her on board!'

'What if she says no?'

Lannec shrugged and went over towards a set of rails that the crane was lowering into the hold. Lenglois had not been gone three minutes before he raised his eyes, climbed up the ladder, strode quickly along the deck and leaned over the mess-room stair.

He got there just in time to hear the cabin door opening and then closing shut.

So the radio operator had been inside!

'Where's the bos'n?' Lannec asked the steward as he went by.

'He went to get a new dressing for his wound this morning. One of the dockhands told him about a healer, and he went off half an hour ago.'

Lannec was talking for the sake of it. In reality he was sick with nerves, waiting to find out what they were saying to each other downstairs.

'How many bottles did we get through last night?'

'Six, including a bottle of chartreuse. Did you know the ladies came back just now? They wanted to come aboard, but I swore to them that you weren't here . . .'

He shrugged his shoulders and did a mental calculation of how long it would take to finish loading. If the stevedores agreed to do overtime, they could be at sea that very evening.

But he would have to pay another call at the harbourmaster's office, and see the health inspector too.

The radio man still hadn't reappeared. Had Mathilde decided to pour her heart out to him? Lannec walked up and down the deck. Moinard came into view.

'What time is high tide?'

'The pilot said that if we can leave at nine we will still have the ebb tide with us. If not, then tomorrow morning . . .'

'Would you mind looking after the paperwork for me?'

He went to see the foreman and promised him a fat bonus if the loading were finished in time.

He would have liked to have ten times more to do. He was boiling with anger. He didn't feel at ease anywhere he was. When he came back on board, he saw Paul Lenglois coming up on deck at last and trying to hide his embarrassment.

'What did she say?'

The poor man was scarlet, and his eyes swivelled everywhere except in front of him. His fingers fiddled with the hem of his jacket.

'She does not want to leave the boat.'

'Did she say why?'

'She did not say why.'

'That's the last straw! Did you explain we were going to get knocked about?'

'I even told her the *Tonnerre-de-Dieu* could go down,' he sighed.

'No need to exaggerate. What's she saying?'

'She's not saying anything.'

Lannec stamped his foot on the metal deck.

'But damn it all! You must have said more than three sentences to each other in the twenty minutes you spent together!'

'I swear . . .'

'She told you I was a monster!'

'No. She said nothing about you.'

'Who did she talk about, then?'

'She didn't talk about anybody . . . About the boat . . . She asked me to bring her a chart and to give her our position on it every day.'

'What did you say?'

'I said I would, provided you agreed to it.'

'That's all?'

Lenglois blushed an even deeper hue. Lannec realized the radio man was beginning to hate him, but he could live with that.

'What's in your pocket?'

'A letter.'

'To whom?'

'I promised to put it in the post without showing it to anyone.'

'Well, damn you!' Lannec said before moving off.

He was all the more fraught for having missed his regular nap, and he'd slept three hours at most the previous night. Night had fallen once more. Arc lights illuminated parts of the quay but left others in pitch black. On board there was a persistent racket that made your ears buzz after a while.

'Shall I go to the harbourmaster's office?' Moinard asked as he went ashore in civilian clothes with the yellow briefcase under his arm.

'Agreed.'

'Should I book the pilot for this evening?'

'You can book the bloody devil for all I care!'

He would rather his wife took ten, twenty, fifty lovers! He would rather be the biggest cuckold in the entire merchant navy.

What he could not accept, what unhinged him completely, what unmanned him entirely was the fact that he did not understand.

'Why the devil is she digging in her heels?'

Even women don't do things for no reason at all. And it was not a life for her to spend weeks shut up in a cabin on a freighter.

He'd interrogated the steward two or three times, and he eventually confessed that she had thrown up.

So what was she hoping for? In Caen, she could have gone back to her weak-chested idiot Marcel.

Lannec marched up and down the deck, leaned over the forward hold, then over the rear hold. He came across Mathias, the chief engineer, and stood right in front of him.

'Do you understand it at all?'

'What?'

'My wife staying on board! There's no way of getting her to go ashore!'

'Perhaps she's jealous,' Mathias ventured.

'How about that! She's jealous, but she cheats on me!'

He went on repeating the jibe as if he enjoyed it. The bos'n got back from his healer, and Lannec motioned him to come up.

'What did he say?'

'He gave me an ointment and a formula to recite.'

'What's the formula for?'

'To recite when I put on the ointment.'

And that was the man who dressed up as a ghost to steal hams from the stores! Maybe he too was scared of spirits or the devil?

'What's she got against me? Hey, take it gently down there . . . You'll damage the cargo battens!'

He didn't feel the cold, which was getting ever sharper as the night drew on. And suddenly, as he walked up and down with his hands in the pockets of his capacious jacket, his fingers lighted on a crumpled piece of paper.

He did not need to read it. It was that disgusting anonymous letter he'd found on the table when they'd left Rouen.

'Don't try to be too clever . . .'

But the *Tonnerre-de-Dieu* had reached her destination all the same! Lannec grinned. Then his laugh evaporated. Maybe it meant he wouldn't get back to his home port, namely Rouen.

He clenched his fists. Was he going to become as gullible as Campois or the bos'n?

'A joker!'

Who else could have written the note? An enemy? But he didn't have any enemies, for heaven's sake! Someone who envied him? But they all did, *tonnerre de Dieu*, all the captains he'd worked for who'd not been able to buy their own boats! Because of the economic crisis the shipping companies were sacking them one after another . . .

But that was no reason to . . .

'What does she want to get out of it?'

And his eyes narrowed, because he was beginning to see a possible connection between Mathilde's obstinacy and that note.

He summoned up names and pictures in his mind: Dame Pitard perched over her shoe shop and running her two blocks of flats like the old miser she was; Marcel, bent over his violin and making gooey eyes at all the sentimental young ladies of Caen; Mathilde, who had not spent twenty complete days with him in two years of marriage and maybe because of that was always fearful of him and treated him almost like a stranger . . .

But that's not a reason to . . .

The foreman of the lading crew came up to him, tipped his cap and asked in broken French:

'French cognac, yes you have?'

He grinned from ear to grimy ear, and Lannec clapped a hand on his shoulder.

'Come with me, Fritz! Let's knock back a glass of well-aged calvados!'

The *Tonnerre-de-Dieu* left her berth just after nine o'clock.

The two clippers were still docked, hoping for another load, and when the French boat was still only half a cable away from them, some stones, bolts and other bits of metal fell on deck, without hurting anyone.

Lannec didn't go to bed until the pilot had disembarked abreast of the Cuxhaven light at three in the morning.

6.

They were three days out of Hamburg, and life on board had changed. From Rouen to the Elbe, the *Goddammit* had sailed from beacon to beacon like a tram going from stop to stop, and there had hardly been time to settle into the voyage

But as it was now impossible to stay out on deck, every member of the crew was inevitably obliged to find his own nook, a place where he could hunker down with his own habits and peculiarities at every hour of the day and night.

In the third century BCE the first Mediterranean explorer to reach this stretch of ocean recorded that he had come to 'those places where land properly speaking no longer exists, nor sea nor air, but a mixture of these things, like a marine lung, in which it is said that earth and water and all things are in suspension'.

Although it was not raining, rivulets of water zigzagged down the side of the black funnel under a colourless sky. The deck was never dry and was in crepuscular shade even at the start of day. The bulkheads, inside and out, were always dripping; and water even dribbled down the stairwell and on to the mess-room floor.

All around the *Tonnerre-de-Dieu* was a universe of cold and white in which from time to time the hazy black shape of a trawler could be seen as if hanging in space, for there was no horizon.

At night unseen ships filled the sea with the persistent sound of sirens.

There were no colours, other than the red band around the funnel and the yellow oilskins of seamen who sometimes had to cross the deck. Everyone wore wood-soled winter boots, rubber gloves, thick knitwear and scarves.

Lannec had a sore throat, probably because he was smoking too much, or because of his wild night in Hamburg. He couldn't settle down. Ten times a day he plodded round his boat from stem to stern in a headstrong and grumpy mood, looking for the right place to be.

Around ten that morning he was once more at a loss. When they were sailing the open sea he had more time on his hands, and Moinard did too, because Monsieur Gilles, the bos'n and even the radio operator took turns on watch.

He shook out his pipe over the side and went down to the mess room, already cross about what he would find down there. He hung his oilskins on the coat-rack as he went past, dragged his feet, sat on the bench near the door and coughed.

Mathilde was there. She'd got a new habit of sitting in the mess room to do her sewing and embroidery, and as a result the green baize was cluttered with bits of thread and silk and pockmarked by stray pins and needles.

The lights were on because you couldn't see well enough to read by the light of day. Moinard was sitting at the other end of the table studying his maths books with a pencil in his hand, writing out equations and formulas on a scrap of paper.

There was nothing surprising about the scene. Moinard wasn't on watch, and so he had to be somewhere. Yet Lannec bristled as if he'd seen something indecent!

When he came across his wife in such a way, they both pretended not to notice each other and didn't exchange a word.

This time Mathilde wasn't sewing but laying out playing cards in columns, thoughtfully. Her husband, who knew the tally of the ship's stores, wondered where the cards came from.

But what was there for him to do? He couldn't simply stay there with his wife on one side and Moinard on the other!

Come to think of it, what did he do with himself on his other voyages, when Mathilde wasn't there? He had no idea. Yet in twenty years at sea, he had never once been bored.

On this voyage, however, it did not feel right! He did not feel at home. His ship didn't feel like a real ship, that was the reason!

He sighed, stood up, grabbed his oilskins and went into the steward's glory hole, where he was greasing a pair of boots.

'Was it you who gave my wife a deck of cards?'

Campois shook his head.

'She didn't ask you for any?'

'I told her the bos'n probably had a pack.'

Lannec went back out into the marine lung, crossed the deck and went up to the bridge, where the bos'n was pacing up and down to keep warm. The light was on up here as well, in front of the steersman with his red nose.

'So she's going to play patience!' Lannec muttered to himself.

He'd never seen his wife reading cards, and it puffed yet more bile into his bad mood.

The bos'n was now free of his bandages, but they had left him with a strange face of shiny, taut skin that he had to powder with talc. For ten minutes and more Lannec watched him without saying anything, something he'd been doing more frequently these last few days. It was as if he was exploring the universe afresh and looking for new meanings in people and things.

'Bos'n, tell me, was it you who gave my wife a deck of cards?'

'She asked me.'

Why did Lannec suddenly imagine the bos'n was making fun of him? Yet his face hadn't moved. Not the slightest trace of a smile on his lips.

'Do you read the cards as well?'

'I'm not very good at it. But my wife is famous for it all round the neighbourhood of Saint-Pierre . . .'

Lannec scowled.

'Saint-Pierre, in Caen? I thought you two had a grocery in Le Havre.'

'Not at all! We've always lived in Caen. What's more, Madame Pitard has been one of my wife's customers for years, and I've known Mademoiselle Mathilde – sorry, I mean the captain's wife – since she was in pigtails.'

'Where's your shop?'

'Between the butcher's and the tobacconist's, five houses on from Madame Pitard's. You've been in many times. Also, your sister-in-law comes in to have her fortune told.'

Lannec was obviously wrong, but he had the distinct impression that the bos'n's eyes were full of the sharpest irony. It was absurd! Despite which, he turned his back and stared at the sea, or rather at the off-white cotton wool through which the *Tonnerre-de-Dieu* made its way with its rhythmic chugging sound.

It wasn't the time of day when he usually thought about Caen, because his memories were essentially of the afternoons. But when all the lights were put on at around four and made haloes in the damp haze, he would suddenly feel his hometown coming back to him. In his mind's eye he could see the Saint-Pierre tram right up against the pavement, the shop windows misted with condensation, and the women from country villages all dressed in black, dragging their offspring from lamp post to lamp post down the street.

That's when he also thought about the Pitard clan, with regret and with remorse.

How had he managed to get involved with that family? All he'd done was drop into Chandivert's of an evening and smile at a girl eating cake and listening to music!

And now he had a mother-in-law, a brother-in-law, a

sister-in-law and a sickly nephew with a rickety leg they were trying to correct by enclosing it in a steel and leather device!

Mathilde had an architect brother, Oscar. Madame Pitard had given him the best apartment in the building.

'Your brother has to receive clients. It is only fair for him to have a better apartment than you do . . .'

But he didn't have any clients, or hardly any. The fact of the matter was that Madame Pitard gave him money to live on, but that didn't prevent her swooning with admiration for her son.

Why did the bos'n have to make him think about those dismal puppets? He could see the Pitard apartment, where they gathered every Sunday, he could hear himself saying, just to fill the time:

'When we were in Holland, where they're Protestants . . .'

Oscar Pitard would interrupt him:

'Holland is not a Protestant country. It is . . .'

'Have you been there?'

'I don't need to go there. I know!'

'You see, Émile, Oscar does know!' Dame Pitard would say. 'You keep on contradicting him, but he's a learned man!'

It was idiotic! Even Mathilde used to put her oar in!

'If Oscar says . . .'

Those weren't memories to be stirred on board a boat. They ruined it all for him. He didn't feel as if he was at sea. He didn't feel at home.

Just to think that Moinard was sitting below opposite Mathilde telling her fortune with playing cards . . .

That was something else he hadn't known! Now the bos'n had told him about his shop, he could see it clearly again. It had an ill-lit, narrow front window, squeezed between two larger shops. It sold everything – vegetables, smoked fish, pickled herring, groceries, and there was even a bar where you could have a drink, for women in Normandy weren't averse to a glass when they were out shopping.

There must have been an overheated back room where the bos'n's wife read cards, and coffee grounds as well.

Old Madame Pitard was a regular! And so was Oscar's wife, an anaemic woman the family disparaged for having given birth to a weakling!

Mathilde must have been a customer too . . .

Whatever put the idea into her head of coming on board? When she first told him of her plan, he thought nothing of it. He'd even felt flattered. He told himself it was out of love, and in any case he didn't think it would last and that one trip would be quite enough.

But now he was more suspicious. He was looking for impossible explanations, and he turned twice towards the loitering bos'n with suspicion in his eyes.

There was a noise on deck, to starboard. He leaned over the balustrade and saw a seaman hauling in a line with an invisible catch thrashing wildly in the water a hundred metres out.

'Ahoy! I need help!' the sailor yelled, for he couldn't manage it on his own.

Nobody heard, so Lannec clattered down the ladder to lend a hand. It was a relief to grab hold of the line, though it could cut his hand, and to grunt:

'Go get the harpoon.'

The beast on the line pulled so hard that Lannec had to lean back on his heels. There was always some sailor who would bait a line with chicken feathers, and now and again a dogfish would bite.

Campois heard the noise and came running. The two of them wound in the line as the sailor held the harpoon up high.

It was warm work, it warmed the body and the soul. Lannec stopped thinking, clenched his teeth, tugged in turn with Campois, and the line cut into the palms of his hands.

'Heave! . . . Ho! . . . Keep in time, Campois!'

The thrashing came closer, and when it was three metres from the side, the sailor stood on the rail and threw the harpoon. It dug into the flesh and stayed upright in the water like a flagpole.

'Tug! . . . Tug! . . .'

After a few minutes' struggle, the three of them could relax and smile, as a two-metre-long rock salmon flopped on to the deck. Its mouth was open and it was bleeding from the side, and it was still flaying about, trying to hit something in the void.

Didn't Lannec sometimes seem like a man who'd been thrown out of his own home? He passed by the bos'n once again, who was still on watch. Then he drank a glass of spirits in the chart house, had a look at the map and, for want of anything else to do, went to see the radio operator.

As he approached the room he heard the clacking of a typewriter. Paul Lenglois had a portable that he used at sea to type up the stories he wrote.

Where Moinard studied Einstein's theories, the radio operator wrote adventure stories for children's magazines.

Lannec pushed the door open.

'Are you working?'

Sometimes he used the familiar form of address with Lenglois and sometimes he was more formal. When he spoke informally, as he did now, it was because he needed friendship, though he wouldn't have admitted it. He sat down on a chair facing the radio equipment.

'What are you writing?'

Lenglois looked as if he felt embarrassed. Lannec noticed a typed sheet lying on the table and picked it up.

The police believe they are on the tail of the Villefranche murderer. The suspect is . . .

Lannec understood it was a news item Lenglois had transcribed from a radio broadcast.

In Rome it has been stated that the airmen . . .

He filled his pipe and let his eyes wander round the room.

'So now you're actually *typing* the news?'

Normally, Lenglois recited the day's events to the other officers at dinner and if anything sensational happened, he would communicate it verbally to the captain.

But these sheets were neatly typed up.

'It's for my wife, isn't it?'

He'd guessed. He pretended to laugh, but he was furious.

'How long have you been providing this service?'

'Since Hamburg. I thought I could . . .'

'Like hell you did!'

Beside the typescript was the pad Lenglois used to take notes on the news broadcasts as they came in. Lannec glanced at them, out of a sense of propriety.

Saõ Paulo de Luanda. – The German freighter *Stadt von Düsseldorf* is on fire thirty miles off the coast of Africa and has been broadcasting distress signals throughout the night. The fire started in a load of raw wool from Australia. At four a.m. the whole crew, less two men unaccounted for, had taken refuge on the forecastle, and the radio operator said he could not hold out much longer as the smoke was so thick he could not see his switchboard. Since then there has been no signal from the *Stadt von Düsseldorf*. The nearest ship is the Delmas Line's *Agen*, but she is still ten or twelve miles away.

Lannec's face was stony. He knew the coast in those parts, on the other side of the Equator, and he'd even sailed on the *Agen*.

He could imagine what it all looked like, in the heat haze of the tropical sun.

'You aren't typing that one up?'

'Probably better not to,' Lenglois muttered. He was getting more timid by the day, as if each day he had more reason to be ashamed.

'Copy it up!'

'You think I should?'

'I'm telling you to! And give it to my wife with the rest of the news.'

His voice betrayed stifled anger. Was he master of this ship, or was he not?

'From now on, you type up all the interesting news items and give them to me to read first.'

He slammed the door shut and stood on the landing deck on his own for a few minutes.

What if the *Tonnerre-de-Dieu* caught fire? Given where they were, it would be less dangerous than in the South Atlantic. To port, the coast of Scotland was barely more than forty miles away, and to starboard Norway was not far either.

You couldn't see anything, neither land nor shipping, but all around the freighter there were other steamers, mostly fishing trawlers, since the herring season had started. They would respond very quickly to an SOS.

Lannec smiled to himself, thinking how stressful Mathilde would find the news from Luanda.

It served her right! Why hadn't she stayed behind in Caen and spent her afternoons fainting over that idiotic Marcel and his violin?

That's what really wound him up: all of them, Marcel no less than Oscar Pitard, were idiots and small-town trash, but they had the gall to poison his happy life!

For he had never been happier than on his departure from

Rouen. At that time, for him, the *Tonnerre-de-Dieu* was the most beautiful boat in the world, despite its funnel, which was as narrow as a stove-pipe and as obsolete as a crinoline.

So what! He was proud of his crinoline! He would prove to anyone who cared to listen that nowadays nobody could build a boat as sturdy and as manoeuvrable as his!

He was happy, *tonnerre de Dieu*! And when he was happy he could talk about anything to anybody with equal enthusiasm and the eloquence that went with it.

The marine lung did not make him sad, or even melancholic, quite the opposite, in fact. He'd been to Archangelsk many times without being bored for a minute. Only, he'd felt he was on his own boat. He had his position. He would smoke his pipe looking vaguely into the distance. Then he would have a glass, read the small ads in a three-week-old newspaper, have a nap for an hour or two, then chat with Tom, Dick or Harry . . .

Days passed so quickly with that routine that it was a real surprise when all of a sudden you found you had arrived at your destination.

To think that Mathilde was in the mess room telling her fortune with playing cards!

Could you imagine that to get to his cabin he had to cross the mess room under the disparaging gaze of his wife?

Because she was the one who did the disparaging!

And she hadn't just brought herself on board, she'd brought the whole Pitard clan – with the Rue Saint-Pierre, the shoe shop, the know-all brother-in-law and his handicapped son, and even the bos'n's wife and her coffee grounds!

He could not get all those images out of his mind. What's more, people were making fun of him and keeping an eye out to stop him from depleting the fortune of the Pitard clan!

That was the reason! He'd made the mistake of requesting a guarantee for the bank loan.

'*Tonnerre de Dieu!*' he suddenly bawled out.

Something else occurred to him. He hadn't paid attention at the right time. It's true that it happened when he was all tied up with buying the ship. He was making trips back and forth between Rouen and England to hold meetings with the sellers and the ship certification people at Bureau Veritas.

'Oscar said something very true,' Dame Pitard had sneered. 'If anything should happen to you, we need to be sure your partner won't be able to take advantage. You never know . . .'

So he'd been obliged to take out a life insurance policy, with a medical exam and a 5,000 franc premium.

'You still have relatives in Brittany. If there were a misfortune, it wouldn't be fair for them to . . .'

So he'd signed another piece of paper that the family notary drew up, which stipulated that on his death all the assets of the marriage would pass to his wife.

'What a joker!' he groaned.

That was something he often said, about anything and everything. It reminded him of the note he'd found on the table, and he shoved his hands deeper into his pockets.

He would not have got angry if someone had stolen money from him. For example, he'd not said anything to the bos'n when he'd tried to steal a ham.

What he could not accept, what drove him mad, was having his pleasure stolen from him! It had taken him too long to have the joy of being master of his own boat to be able to pass it up.

'What is it?' he grunted as he saw the radio operator coming up to him.

'A trawler is requesting us to give him a one-mile berth, because of his nets.'

'Did you hear that, bos'n?'

'One point to port!' the bos'n ordered the steersman, for he still used the old language of sail.

'Did you give my wife the news?'

Paul Lenglois nodded.

With his hands in pockets and his pipe between his teeth, Lannec gave himself the treat of going down to the mess room to find his wife and Moinard poring over a map together.

It was the big track chart of the South Atlantic. Moinard was using a pencil to point to the place where the burning freighter was about to go down.

Lannec chuckled loud enough to be heard. Mathilde raised her eyes and looked at the captain with the icy stare she would have given an intruder. The table was cluttered with maps and maths books. Campois was in the gangway, waiting to lay the table for dinner.

Lannec went to his cabin, took off his oilskins, sighed, and kicked off his boots. He massaged his over-hot feet and then put on carpet slippers.

The sharp change in temperature made blood rush to his head. Over his bunk there was a photograph of Mathilde that had accompanied him on all his voyages these past two years.

He shrugged his shoulders, cast his mind back to Rue Saint-Pierre, imagined he could see the haughty figure of Dame Pitard sneaking into the grocery shop, trying to keep up appearances yet needing a soothsayer to advise her.

Come to think of it, who had taken on the bos'n? He couldn't recall. The last weeks on shore had been chaotic. Moinard had the job of hiring part of the crew.

Lannec hadn't switched on the lamp, and his cabin was as murky as dirty water at the bottom of a flask. He sat on the edge of his bunk and drew on an unlit pipe, letting figures pass before his mind's eye. They didn't seem to be in any particular order and yet they were connected to each other in ways he couldn't quite grasp.

'When Oscar can get on with building his great monument . . .' Dame Pitard was saying . . .

. . . and the lad with his leg wrapped in leather and shiny steel, a poor boy of four with a head too big for his twisted body . . .

. . . and his sister-in-law who'd bought a fur coat that made Mathilde jealous . . .

. . . and the bos'n who played at ghosts . . .

He stood up, stretched and then turned to the mirror and yelled at himself:

'A plague on them all!'

7.

The air was so still and the grey so intense that you could separate the dots of light from the dots of dark, and it made you want to make them run through your fingers like grains of sand.

Lannec's oilskins were hanging on the coat-rack behind the enamelled door, and now and again a drop of water fell from them on to the linoleum floor.

The captain's watch hung on a nail near his head. He only had to open one eye to see the dial and the hands, and he could hear the racing pulse of his little silver device.

A slower and stronger pulse overlaid it – the sound of the engine going full steam ahead.

And on top of that there was the rocking of the sea, at times gentle and slow, at other times jagged and fast.

They had passed through Fair Isle Channel at night, in the howling noise of wind and backwash, and now the *Tonnerre-de-Dieu* was riding waves six to seven metres high, falling into such steep-sided troughs that the freight in the hold rattled around like nails in a tin.

Lannec was having a snooze after spending sixteen hours on the bridge. The wind and the cold had at long last given him a mild temperature, which he savoured in his drowsy state, licking his blistered lips with his tongue.

The radiator next to his bunk gave off great waves of heat, and the cabin's two portholes were covered in condensation.

He felt really comfortable in the melting warmth of the

cabin, listening to the full-throated rumble of the engine keeping time with Atlantic rollers . . .

Now and again Lannec thought in pictures, and the violent contrast between the cold and the warmth was probably what brought back his memory of Honningsvåg, a Norwegian village far beyond North Cape, on the Arctic Sea. He smiled with his eyes closed. He felt hotter. He thought he was once again on his way to deliver coal to Archangelsk and going ashore for an unscheduled port call at Honningsvåg.

It was deepest winter. They had been sailing for four days in the polar night, but there they were, all of a sudden, putting in at a wooden jetty lit by powerful electric lights.

Other lights shone in all the windows of the little houses dotted around a snow-covered mountain slope.

It was as magical as a Nordic Yuletide or a German nativity scene.

Children dressed in furs slid headlong down the slope on skis and came to a perfect halt right at the side of the black ship. Little sleds hauled by small horses that didn't look real ran around in all directions.

Lannec went ashore and wandered around with his hands in pockets as if in a dream. On the right-hand side of the street was a hairdressing salon, a hairdressing salon that looked like a toy. Everybody's noses were red and cold. Beneath your feet the snow crackled like new shoes.

And coming from far away where there were few lights to be seen, Lannec could make out the sound of music, and he went up to a house that seemed warmer than the others. He went in and was instantly enveloped in the 'Blue Danube' played on violins, on a gramophone record.

There was a smell of cake, spirits and tea. A man in a fur coat was sitting at a table opposite a girl with a mane of hair who was smiling as she listened to him.

There were other women, from Hungary, to take care of him and pour him a drink, as they stammered out a few words of French . . .

Didn't he have to leave by the back door after he'd spent a long while in a room with one of the girls?

And in Iceland, he'd . . .

That memory was sharper, with a stronger contrast between light and dark. In the middle of the picture was a factory chimney, then . . .

He pricked up his ears. The tick-tock of his watch and the rumble of the engine were still there with him, but he suddenly became aware of a strange rhythm. He furrowed his brow, still without opening his eyes. He wasn't asleep. He was drowsing, he was sweating under the sheets, and his limbs were like jelly.

The noise wasn't in his cabin. It wasn't coming from the deck, either.

It took him a while to realize that there was whispering going on in the mess room next door. Or rather, people talking in half-tones. They were talking non-stop. Someone was making an interminably long speech.

It was Mathilde! She was spoiling everything yet again! He forgot Honningsvåg. He strained to hear. He even raised his head from the pillow in the hope of making out what was being said.

Who could she be talking to? And what was she talking about? Her mother was capable of complaining for hours on end without getting tired. If she had to, she would go back to her marriage, her first confinements, her husband's death and all the disasters her tenants had inflicted on her . . .

Lannec turned over in bed in the hope of sinking back into numbness. But the voice pursued him, a voice as monotonous as those you hear at vespers when you pass by a convent . . .

Moinard was on watch. Lenglois must be at his switchboard

with his headphones on. Mathilde didn't deign to confide in the steward.

Lannec turned over again, opened his eyes, stirred and propped himself on his elbow. At times he thought he could distinguish the words being spoken, for the sound was sharp enough, but the toneless rigmarole made no sense.

It was getting even darker. The black dots in the foggy air now outnumbered the light ones. Suddenly Lannec got up, pulled up his trousers over his hips and found his carpet slippers on the rug with his feet.

He was really tired. His eyes were puffy, and the first draw on his pipe seemed less appealing than it usually did. He leaned towards the bulkhead as he put on his jacket, but to no avail, for though the voice sounded louder there, the words were still a jumble.

He opened the door abruptly. The lights in the mess room weren't on, which made it seem closeted and intimate. Mathilde was sitting on a corner of the bench seat with her elbows on the table, and the bos'n was standing by the bulkhead and leaning on it with his shoulders.

'Get out!' Lannec ordered.

He even gave the man a push because he wasn't moving fast enough. He shut the door to the gangway and then, seeing his wife make a move that suggested she meant to go back to her cabin, he went over to the other door, turned the key in the lock and put it in his pocket.

He hadn't spoken a word to Mathilde for five days and now he felt like doing so. He sat down opposite her and without thinking went straight to the point.

'What were you telling him?' he grunted.

As he hadn't had his habitual milky coffee, his stomach was uneasy, and his mouth tasted stale. He stood up to turn the switch so as to see his wife in the light.

'I'm waiting! What were you telling the bos'n?'

He'd had enough! The radio operator, then Moinard, now the bos'n . . . everybody was in on it!

'You were whining, weren't you? You were complaining about having married a brute . . .'

His narrow eyes had already noticed signs of seasickness on Mathilde's face. She was pale, and there were two yellowish creases on each side of her nose.

But she did not avert her eyes. She waited with calm self-confidence, and her steadiness made her look like the accuser, not the accused.

'Whatever you may think, I am the master on board, do you understand that? I do not like you telling stories to the men under my command!'

He sat down again. Images of Honningsvåg still flitted across his mind, but they dissipated as quickly as a morning mist.

'Will you answer me?'

'I have nothing to say.'

She had said something! It was the first time in a long while. Lannec had almost forgotten the sound of her voice.

'Really! You have nothing to say! And I suppose you think you are a victim?'

She looked at the locked door and sighed.

'That's right! You are a prisoner! And let me tell you right away that you have to give an explanation. I've had enough! I've had it up to the back teeth!'

He'd coped for a long time, but he'd been driven out of his mind by the last straw, that droning voice on the other side of the bulkhead while he lay idly dreaming . . .

One thing disturbed him, however, and that was the way his wife was staring at him. She was calm, to be sure. But she was posing like a person who had nothing to hide.

Yet there was something pained in her eyes – but it was the

trace of a physical pain. As if she was scared of being hit again. She followed every one of her husband's gesticulations. When he made to stand up, she raised her hands as if to ward off a blow.

'It won't take long!' Lannec muttered as he turned away. 'Doesn't stop it being time for an explanation. Will you tell me the reason why you have insisted on staying on board?'

She didn't budge an inch and kept her mouth shut.

'In Rouen, I didn't think anything of it. Like the good-hearted fool that I am, I thought it was a token of your affection. Mind you, I knew that life on board was not possible for a woman, but I expected you to see that yourself after a few days.'

She kept her eyes on him, while he sought in vain to see in Mathilde's figure and tense expression the girl he'd fallen in love with and taken in his arms so many times of an evening in the empty streets of Caen, in doorways and in the shadows of the harbour buildings.

'Answer!'

'I have nothing to answer for.'

'What are you doing here?'

'You know that very well.'

'Eh?'

He stood up again and paced up and down the mess room with his hands behind his back.

'Will you please explain yourself?'

'Don't play the fool.'

Now that was her mother's voice, the voice of the whole Pitard clan looking down on the world from their two blocks of flats with imperturbable self-satisfaction.

'Do you mean you had had enough of your Marcel?'

She didn't bat an eyelid. She sat on in the corner, where her woollen bodice made a red splash.

'Marcel never beat me up.'

'*Tonnerre de Dieu*, he never married you either!'

'Because Mother didn't want him to.'

'Well, well! Now you're getting talkative all of a sudden. Maybe you'll soon tell me just what you're doing here.'

'It's not worth the breath.'

At times like that Lannec could be oddly self-controlled. He could feel anger rising in him and he knew it would explode, but only when he wanted it to. He held himself back, clenched his fists behind his back and cast a sideways glance at his wife.

'Look, Mathilde, I'm still keeping calm . . .'

'I'm becoming accustomed to getting hit.'

He took a deep breath and came to a halt in the middle of the room.

'I am asking you why you are here. For the love of God, listen to me and don't make me do something terrible . . .'

He was almost beside himself. Mathilde was scared and shrank into her corner. She said again:

'You know full well.'

'What do I know? If one of us two is going crazy, it's time to know which it is!'

'Not I.'

'Answer the question!'

'Do you really want me to?'

'Do I have to go down on bended knee? Then I will! I can't stand this a minute longer!'

'What were you planning to do with the *Tonnerre-de-Dieu*?'

Then all of a sudden his anger subsided, as did his fever, and everything else. He was like a punctured balloon, with a look of astonishment in his child-like, innocent eyes.

'I don't understand.'

'You would say that!'

He went up to her slowly.

'Explain yourself! Tell me what's in your mind . . .'

She recoiled. He grabbed one of her wrists and clutched it violently.

'Confess, Émile!'

She smiled maliciously. She was putting on a show of condescension.

'Confess, now I know everything!'

'Confess what?'

He was looking her straight in the eye, with his face almost touching hers.

'You found a shipment for Iceland at the drop of a hat, didn't you? Was that a coincidence? Weren't you expecting it?'

She was taunting him, the hussy! She was putting on airs and graces!

'I found a shipment. So what?'

'You are telling me that it wasn't prearranged?'

'No, it was not!'

'That's a lie!'

He shook her and then let go.

'Look, just because we are the Pitards, and my father ran a shoe shop doesn't mean you can take us for idiots. We were tipped off! I knew what you planned to do with your boat . . .'

'And what was that?'

'To sell it in America or some other place and then run off with one of your lady friends! Iceland is halfway there . . .'

Lannec sat down and rubbed his brow vigorously. There was a long pause as the captain tried to sort things out in his mind.

'One moment . . .' he said as his wife made to stand up. 'You were Marcel's lover . . . Do you still admit that?'

'I do!'

'OK! So you were told or you imagined that I wanted to sell the boat and live overseas . . . On the strength of that, you drop your lover and set sail with me . . .'

'So?'

'So nothing. It's consistent. You are my natural heiress. What's more, your mother guaranteed bank loans to the tune of two hundred thousand francs.'

He was frighteningly calm, and Mathilde was scared.

'I said, don't move! We haven't finished. Don't be afraid. I'm not even going to hit you.'

His eyes were as narrow as slits and very still.

'I just want to know who told you all this nonsense.'

'I can't do that.'

'You've no option but to tell me. Maybe I've looked like a puppet on strings up to now, but I would like you to know that . . .'

'Will you give me back my cabin key?'

'Who told you that story? Admit it, it was your mother . . .'

'My mother's as good as yours, and we don't have to slip her six hundred francs a month either . . .'

He didn't flinch. He got up slowly, went to the cabin door and opened it.

Now it was her turn not to want to end the conversation. She stayed in the mess room as if she'd not understood what her husband had done. He didn't even hate her! She was a Pitard, that was all! He'd been wrong!

'Go to bed.'

There was a knock at the door and a voice from the gang-way called out:

'Captain!'

'What is it?'

Lenglois mumbled uncertainly:

'There's a message . . .'

Lannec unlocked the door, saw the radio operator looking upset, took the transcript he'd brought down and read it:

SOS In distress latitude 60° 42′ longitude . . .

He suddenly relaxed, with instant relief. Lannec had no eyes for his wife. In a blink she had ceased to exist, and he looked at the compass on the mess-room ceiling that allowed him to keep track of the ship's course from below deck.

He read the rest of the telegram.

'Who is the *Françoise*?'

'A trawler out of Fécamp. Twenty-eight hands on board . . .'

'Any more information?'

'They hit something. They think it was a derelict . . .'

Lannec spelled it out:

Longitude 5° 30′ 15″ west of Greenwich meridian.

'Get back to your headphones!' he ordered Lenglois.

'Excuse me! What's happening?' Mathilde interrupted.

Lenglois hovered in anguish, uncertain whether to stay to answer the question or to obey the captain's command.

'Move a leg!' the skipper bawled. Then he turned to his wife, whose face was hard but firm, almost serene.

'What's happening? Twenty-eight men who have nothing to do with the Pitard clan and who are going to go down!'

Upon which, he too went out, grabbing his oilskins and his sou'wester on the way. He pulled them on as he rushed across the dark and slippery deck. He had to walk sideways because of the roll. By the time he got to the bridge his hands and face were drenched.

He couldn't see Moinard at first in the dark, but he could make out the face of the steersman by the feeble light of the compass lamp. He was staring straight ahead, and his mouth was taut. There was nothing to be seen at sea apart from wind-driven waves breaking into white horses as far as the horizon.

A shape emerged from the dark, and Moinard's voice could be heard:

'Well?'

'We'll go.'

'She's thirty-two miles away . . . Maybe other steamers have managed . . .'

The rule is that the ship nearest an accident has to provide assistance.

'Isn't the *Françoise* Jallu's boat?'

'Yes! He's skippering her himself . . .'

Lannec went into the chart house and began by downing a large glass of spirits. Then he leaned over the map with pro-tractor and pencil in hand and drew a line across it to where the sinking trawler was.

'Three points west!' he shouted through the door.

What had his wife meant? What was this story about selling the boat in America?

He went back to the steersman with an appearance of calm and came across Moinard. The mate was grave and hesitated before saying in a low voice:

'We only have four days left . . .'

It was true. It was what the charter party said. The *Tonnerre-de-Dieu* had just four days to reach Reykjavik, failing which they would have to pay a penalty for each day's delay to the company that had chartered them.

'I knew Jallu when he captained ships in the Bordes line,' Lannec replied. 'I even served as his first mate.'

They were young, then! Neither of them had a boat or a wife!

Lannec tottered down to the radio room, and he was soaking wet by the time he got there.

'Any news?'

Lenglois gestured at him to keep quiet. He was wearing headphones, taking notes, turning dials and sending out a message of his own.

'What exactly happened to them? How are they faring?'

Another pause. Then, not ceasing to listen in to the radio signals, Lenglois wrote on a scrap of paper:

The *Françoise* has lost her rudder. She's reporting waves eight metres high and nil visibility. We are the first to answer her call . . .

Lannec bounded back up to the bridge.

'Full steam ahead!' he commanded.

It would take four hours for them to reach the lost trawler. It was not a good course. The beam wind and the swell hit the *Tonnerre-de-Dieu* from the side and made her pitch.

Lannec was already back down with Lenglois, who was transcribing messages one after another.

The ship has lost its steering and is drifting . . . The bos'n has vanished, probably knocked over the side by a wave.

The *Tonnerre-de-Dieu*'s hull rattled with the throb of the engines on full power.

'Did you tell them we're coming?'

Lenglois nodded, frowned and twiddled the dials.

'Well?'

Silence. Both men stayed still. Only Lenglois' finger moved as he tapped the Morse button.

'Nothing?'

The radio operator didn't say anything. Blue sparks came from the transmitter.

'I keep on calling,' Paul mumbled. 'And I'm sure I'm on the right wavelength.'

'No response?'

'Hang on . . .'

He started writing. But it was a message from another ship

much further away from the disaster than the *Tonnerre-de-Dieu*, saying it was not going to change course.

'Are they still off air?'

Lenglois didn't take off his headphones but spoke very loud so as to be able to hear his own words.

'You know what must have happened?' he shouted. 'I can guess, because I know those kinds of boat. The radio room, which is just behind the funnel, must have been washed away . . .'

Through the porthole there was nothing but dark to be seen, and the sky was even blacker than the sea.

'Keep listening. Carry on telling them we're on our way.'

Lannec went back to his command post. As he went out he was blinded by the darkness, which hit him like a wall.

'They've gone quiet,' he said to Moinard.

Then he turned his head, because he thought he saw a lighter shape. It was his wife, wedged upright in a corner of the bridge to keep her from being pushed about by the ship's roll.

8.

Lannec stood stock still for a quarter of an hour, staring at a sea which was getting heavier by the minute. The bridge was dark save for the faint light from the compass, which barely illuminated the steersman's hand. All sounds were drowned out by the roaring of the waves, and only a sixth sense told you if anyone else was nearby.

The closest was the bos'n, whose pipe sent out puffs of smoke that sometimes got as far as Lannec; further on was the long, thin silhouette of Monsieur Gilles.

Moinard was in the chart house, calculating the tightest course to get to the *Françoise*.

The ship was rolling from side to side, and spray sometimes spattered the window of the bridge. At one point Lannec thought he heard a call and pricked up his ears, but it took a few seconds before he saw the radio operator appear.

'Captain! Come quickly . . .'

He'd rushed out of the radio room without taking time to put on oilskins and he was hunched over in comical fashion to protect himself from the squalls of icy water.

When Lannec reached him, he said:

'You understand German, don't you? There's a boat, the *See-teufel*, that's been sending radio messages for the last five minutes, and I can't understand a word . . .'

The radio room was warm and well lit, and when Lannec sat

down in front of the equipment and grabbed the headphones he intuited that in the corner, in the only armchair in the room, sat his wife. It didn't disturb him. At the most his upper lip curled into a sneer. She'd sought out the best spot; so let her stay there.

'I can't hear anything,' he said, turning towards Lenglois.

'Hang on! Their little speech comes round every three or four minutes. It begins with something like *Wir können nicht . . .*'

They hung on, quite still. With the door closed, silence reigned – silence in the cabin, and silence in the unbounded universe to which the headphones gave access. Lannec looked straight ahead with a very calm stare, and nobody could have guessed what was going through his mind. Lenglois had given him his usual seat and was standing up and checking the position of a lever.

Even without headphones, he and Mathilde clearly heard a click and saw Lannec's eyes narrow with concentration. Someone was speaking. A voice was coming from somewhere out there. The skipper furrowed his brow and frowned, trying to understand, while his right hand wrote out the following:

We are five or six miles from the *Françoise* but we have our nets out, and the sea is getting rougher. We cannot move. A piece of wreckage has just hit our side and we think it is an empty lifeboat.

The same identical spoken message was repeated three, then four times. It was a rough voice that made it sound as if the *Seeteufel*'s announcer was in a black rage.

Lannec got up and gave Lenglois his seat back. He checked that nobody was calling them on other wavelengths.

'A while ago I had an English boat signalling in Morse but I'll have to look up her call sign in the code book . . .'

With the headphones on he pulled over a thick volume with a broken spine and thumbed through frantically.

'Here it is . . . It's the *Glynn* . . . Fifteen hundred tons . . .'

'Where is she?'

'I'll call her up.'

There were crackling noises, and sparks flew. Lannec was leaning on the doorjamb; he kept his eyes off his wife but he could guess that she looked worn out.

Lenglois called the English ship through the air. It must be sailing somewhere in those waters.

'Not answering?'

Lenglois began to write, or rather, to make lines of dots and dashes.

'A Norwegian ship is answering! The *Flynderbord*, under Captain Rasmussen, a few miles south of Faroe. He's making six knots and will take ten hours to reach the *Françoise* . . .'

While Lenglois tried to raise the *Glynn* one more time, Lannec went out and braved the storm to get back to the bridge.

You couldn't tell if the water was coming from the sky or the sea. As the ship neared Papa Bank, one of the most vicious sandbanks in the North Atlantic, the troughs got huger still, and even Lannec had to hang on to the railing.

When he got to the bridge Moinard was back on watch. He turned to the captain but didn't say a word.

'There are three or four other ships in the area,' the captain declared. 'The closest to the *Françoise* is a German trawler, but she's dragging her nets.'

Both men knew what that meant: a million francs' worth of netting that held the boat down as firmly as an anchor, and which would take several hours to raise.

'They think they saw an empty lifeboat. At the moment Paul is trying to contact an English ship on the radio.'

He wiped his hands and face, grabbed the bottle of brandy and took a swig, passed it on to Moinard, then to the bos'n.

'We'll be too late,' Moinard declared.

It was part of his character always to do what he was supposed to do steadfastly, even punctiliously, but without giving
any sign of enthusiasm or even belief in it.

You could not see a thing. There were no lights on the horizon, and Lannec ordered the fog horn to be sounded at regular
intervals. He couldn't stay still for very long and after a glance
at the compass he went back to Lenglois, who was startled,
because he was in the middle of a conversation with Mathilde.

'Well then! What about the *Glynn*?'

'Not responding.'

'Are you sure she's in range?'

'Absolutely.'

'Still no peep from the *Françoise*?'

A moment later Lannec was back with Moinard and said to
him quietly:

'The *Glynn*'s backed out!'

They both understood. The ship had no wish to waste time
hunting for a trawler, so it was playing dead and would get
away with it by claiming its transmitter had broken down.

'And your wife?'

'What about my wife?'

'Nothing.'

She was sick, of course she was! She was green with fright.
So what? All the same Lannec would rather he hadn't seen her
in Lenglois' room. Seeing her there each time he went in, sitting in the wicker chair and glaring at him with suspicious
eyes, really got on his nerves.

Because now he had understood! What had been irritating
him since Hamburg or even since Rouen was that vague but
unrelenting suspiciousness in his wife's eyes.

He leaned forwards and could just make out the seamen who
had gathered on the forecastle deck and were straining their
eyes to see something in the dark.

'The men of the *Françoise* can't have managed to improvise a rudder,' he stated.

Nor was it possible to cast a drogue and heave to in such a rough sea.

'How long has he had his own boat?'

'Four years. He'd just bought it the last time I was in Fécamp.'

Jallu had five or six children, Lannec recalled. People teased him about it. He also remembered that because of his numerous offspring Jallu had once put in an application to be a river pilot or a harbourmaster. But as he didn't have any strings to pull, they kept him waiting too long for an answer. And that was why . . .

'Can you see anything?'

The two men stared hard at a spot on the horizon where Lannec thought he had seen a light, but it was just an illusion.

'I can't see anything, but I can hear something!' Moinard grunted.

Both of them heard it at the same time. A cable had snapped, and a metallic object was skipping from one side of the hold to the other at each roll of the ship.

'Bos'n! Get down to the hold with some of the men!'

'Can I have another dram first?'

The bos'n wasn't in a jolly mood.

'Have you worked out the drift?' the captain asked his first mate. 'It must be eight degrees at least . . .'

'We won't find anything.'

'So what?'

Was Moinard backing off the hunt for the *Françoise*?

'So nothing. I was just saying . . .'

The steersman kept his eye on the compass and was constantly shifting the wheel to keep the *Tonnerre-de-Dieu* on course despite the heavy seas on the beam.

It would take another two hours, maybe more. Lannec had

settled into a corner of the bridge with his face to the wind-screen. He turned round in a temper when he felt someone coming up in his back. It was Campois, with a steaming bowl in his hand.

'Have you seen madame?'

'The devil take madame, do you hear me?'

Everyone was looking after Mathilde – even that brute Campois, who'd made her a bowl of broth when nobody had told him to do so!

'With Lenglois,' he added after a pause, by way of correction.

His mind wandered to the white cliffs of Fécamp, its casino on the dyke, then, by association of ideas, to Riva-Bella, where his mother-in-law owned a seaside cottage.

However had he come to spend his honeymoon there? Yet he had, and worn white flannels, an unbuttoned shirt and espadrilles to go and sit under a red-striped parasol on the beach with the whole Pitard clan!

He had even taught his flabby-breasted and bony-hipped sister-in-law how to swim!

'Moinard.'

The first mate stepped up in the dark.

'Go down and see how they're getting on.'

He was listening to the noise from the hold and he felt worried. It must have been a large item that had come adrift. It was imperative to get it tied down, whatever the cost.

He knew all about loose cargo! When he was still a second mate on a Baltic run, he'd seen barrels of wine break out and career in crazy patterns across the deck as if they were hunting men down. The seamen ran away screaming for their lives! One of them had a leg crushed.

'Gilles! Go and have a look in the radio room. Actually, no, stay here. I'll go down . . .'

He opened the door abruptly and cast his eyes around for his wife, who was still seated, but leaning forwards and vomiting into a bucket. The radio operator was at his listening post.

'Nothing new?'

'Fécamp coastguard is asking for details. They've told Jallu's wife, and she's sitting there next to the transmitter.'

'And the *Glynn*?'

'Playing dead!'

'The Norwegian?'

'Requests to be informed if we complete the rescue, in which case she will resume her normal course.'

There was a whole notepad covered in dots and dashes. Lannec glanced at his wife, who had hiccups, and didn't seem to notice he was there. The bowl of broth hadn't been touched and stood on the table next to the radio equipment.

'Keep on giving our position . . . You never know . . . Their transmitter's out of action, but maybe they can still receive . . .'

They could only wait. Back on the bridge there was nothing for Lannec to do but look straight ahead. He heard the men shutting one of the hold battens, and a few minutes later Moinard was back beside him.

'Milou has crushed his finger . . . I've had him put in my quarters.'

'Who's Milou?'

'The tall one with a stutter . . . Three axles had come adrift. We stowed them as best we could.'

Who could have told Mathilde that he wanted to resell the *Tonnerre-de-Dieu* in America and stay there to live? He didn't know whether to laugh or cry. All the same he sensed that Mathilde was sincere. Someone had made up the story and told her. But why?

'You see anything?'

He thought he'd seen a green light. They weren't sure about it, but after fifteen minutes of watching out, there it was, clearly visible. Lannec rushed down to the radio room.

'Ask the boat afore who she is . . .'

Crackling. Sparks. Mathilde, still in the armchair, had closed her eyes.

'She's answering?'

'Not yet.'

Mathilde opened her eyes and looked at Lannec with an expression that conveyed no feelings whatever apart from exhaustion.

He almost felt sorry for her and nearly picked her up to carry her to her cabin, but just at that moment there was an answer on the wireless.

'It's the German boat . . . Do you want to listen?'

The *Seeteufel* had seen them. Her telegraphist was shouting into his mouthpiece with the same gravelly accent as before to give a wide berth, at least a mile and a half, because of their nets.

All they saw of the trawler was that green lantern, then a white one, because you could not even make out the black mass of its hull in the darkness of the night.

'All hands on deck,' Lannec ordered Moinard as he took over command on the bridge. 'A hundred francs' bonus to the first man to see the *Françoise*.'

He filled his pipe, took a swig at the bottle of spirits and checked that the steersman hadn't fallen asleep at the wheel.

They were dead over Papa Bank and could come upon the wreck at any minute. It was piercing cold. Lannec had got water in his boots, and his sore throat was getting steadily worse.

Nobody thought of eating. On the other hand, everybody indulged freely in calvados, and Campois had to bring up another bottle.

The crackling of the wireless could be heard now and again, and it made Lannec think of the Fécamp coastguard's office, with Jallu's wife in the corner, presumably with her eldest beside her, a lad of sixteen. Not far away was Café Léon, where the men of the cod and herring fleets liked to gather, in an aroma of coffee laced with brandy.

The door must have been constantly opening and closing as people came and went fetching news. Everybody there knew what a gale on Papa Bank was like, and most of them knew Lannec as well. They'd just been told he was on the job.

On the *Tonnerre-de-Dieu*, nobody was saying a word, but all were standing quite still with eyes trained on the horizon and hoping to make out a blacker or lighter shape in the darkness.

'Blast the siren!' Lannec ordered.

Was it just an echo? After the first blasts it seemed as if another siren was answering, but nobody could tell what bearing it had.

'Look further north,' the *Seeteufel*'s man bawled into the mouthpiece.

They scoured the darkness to the north, they scoured it to the south, to the east and west, and nearly snagged the German's nets because they'd gone round in a circle without realizing it. The *Françoise* had to be somewhere nonetheless. Now and again they had the distinct impression they could hear her horn. The *Tonnerre-de-Dieu* rushed off towards her but, finding only the empty sea, turned round again.

'Fire a rocket!'

Moinard took charge of the operation with all due caution, because he had once seen a rocket explode in one of his officer's hands. The light it threw up in the sky was hazy because of the humidity, but a few seconds later a similar glow could be seen to starboard.

The engine was put on half-steam. Lannec took the wheel himself. Seeing Mathilde come up behind him, he shouted:

'You can go to bed, you can!'

He didn't check whether she did as she was told. His teeth

were clenched on the stem of his pipe as he leaned forwards with his tense eyes looking out for all they were worth.

'Blast!'

The siren reverberated for a long time as if it were a promise and a foreboding of success. This time the answer they heard was not an echo, but another boat.

'Moinard, did you hear that?'

'Another point to starboard,' Moinard yelled, for the noise made it hard for them to hear each other.

Suddenly, something hove into view: a black mass so near that the *Tonnerre-de-Dieu* had to veer away to avoid hitting it. They were less than a cable-length from it. The swell pushed the two boats so close at times that a collision became a distinct risk.

'Can you make out anyone on board?'

'No. The trawler is almost on its side.'

'Should we launch the lifeboat?'

Nobody spoke. Every man knew what it meant to launch a small boat at night in waves seven or eight metres high. Even Lannec backed off the idea.

'Use the light signals! Tell them we'll pass to starboard and throw them a line . . .'

In all this he still managed to fill his pipe, light up, notice his wife and give her an order:

'Go to bed, *tonnerre de Dieu!*'

She didn't budge. She stood there as if glued to the bulkhead, upright but inert, like a moon in the night.

'Is the tow-line ready?' Lannec asked the deckhands.

'Standing by!'

The wave hit the ship so hard that one side of the boat was waterlogged. Despite the roar of the ocean, they all reckoned they could hear voices, and it was almost like a hallucination. They knew it was actually possible, because the human voice can sometimes travel great distances at sea. They could imagine the men of the *Françoise* transfixed by the *Tonnerre-de-Dieu*'s lights.

'Stand by!'

Lannec clenched his teeth so hard they made dents in his pipe stem. He wanted to pass so close as to almost touch the *Françoise*. The current could easily have thrown his boat on to the wreck, and he used every muscle in his body to hold the wheel on course.

The trawler grew larger. You could clearly see that it had a frightening list. They thought they could distinguish faces and human forms on the forecastle; someone pointed out that it had lost its funnel.

'Cast the tow-line!'

'Cast the tow-line,' Moinard repeated.

'Cast the tow-line,' Monsieur Gilles echoed.

Then silence. The line hadn't reached the trawler's deck, and the operation had to be done all over again.

They tried once again, then a second and third time. The *Françoise* seemed to be listing more and more to starboard. The narrow-hulled trawler pitched and yawed at incredible angles on the crests of the waves.

'Cast the tow-line!'

The storm was still filling the air with its thunderous roar, and yet everyone heard a sigh of relief. It's true that everyone gave a sigh. The cable had hit something hard. Lannec ordered:

'Full steam astern!'

Now the voices on board the *Françoise* were no auditory illusions. They could be heard quite distinctly. You could even guess what was being said, what orders were being given.

'Is that it?'

Lannec turned round once more and cast a venomous stare at his wife, who hadn't moved.

'Dead slow forwards!'

The steel tow-line took up the slack, but the *Tonnerre-de-Dieu* had only gone a hundred metres when the line snapped with a noise that sounded like an explosion.

The rest of the night was unspeakable. They had to wait it out until dawn before they could try anything else. Using the lights, they asked the *Françoise*:

'Can you hold out for a few hours?'

Answer: 'We can try.'

'Have you lost a lifeboat?'

'Six men put to sea in a lifeboat.'

'It must have capsized, because it's been found empty. The radio operator?'

'Swept overboard with the radio cabin and the funnel.'

'Are you taking water?'

'Not a lot. Try to get a message to my wife in Fécamp.'

'She's at the coastguard.'

Every word translated into Morse by light took minutes to transmit, and coding mistakes often got in the way.

In Lenglois' cabin, Lannec was giving dictation:

'From the *Tonnerre-de-Dieu* to Fécamp coastguard . . . We are aside the *Françoise* and hope to rescue her at dawn . . .'

'And all hands alive?' Lenglois queried, who hadn't stood down since the start.

'No, you idiot!'

'What should I add?'

'Nothing.'

Other wives must have joined Madame Jallu at the wireless station by now and must be asking the radio operator the same question.

'They'll find out soon enough.'

Everybody stayed on duty. From one minute to the next a single wave could bring the men of the *Françoise* into even greater peril.

'Will you or will you not go to bed?' Lannec shouted, putting his face right next to his wife's.

He did not want to slack off, yet he felt pity for her as she shrank humbly into herself. He imagined her eyes betrayed admiration, as it were, or a great wish to submit.

'Campois! Take my wife to her bed . . .'

You could hardly stand upright in the wild rolling of the boat on the crests of the waves. Towards two in the morning, five men had to run after carriage wheels that had once again broken free in the hold.

Lannec took his watch out of his pocket from time to time. Dawn would break around 7.30. They were drifting away from the *Françoise*, and then back again. They started chatting to each other.

'Are you holding out?'

'Men are taking turns at the bilge pump. We've switched off the lights as a precaution.'

To prevent an explosion, if water should get into the engine! The *Tonnerre-de-Dieu*'s stokers also put in a few appearances on deck to fill their lungs with spray-laden fresh air.

As they circled around they saw the *Seeteufel* a dozen times, and each time Lenglois called the captain down, because the German telegraphist with the guttural accent kept on asking for news and repeating his warning to give their nets a wide berth.

9.

The sign of the dawning of day on board the *Tonnerre-de-Dieu* was the distribution of black coffee in tin mugs, except for the officers, who got theirs in bowls from the ghostly steward.

'Get a bottle of rum and give all hands a dram,' Lannec said as he glanced at the dawning sky with bad-tempered eye.

It was colder than during the night, and the chill was damp and piercing. All the men had eyes red from fatigue. The sea didn't abate, quite the opposite, and as the greying light allowed more of the *Françoise* to be seen, the men's faces looked glummer still.

The drifting trawler was a sinister sight. Having lost its funnel and bridge, it no longer looked like a proper ship, and it hadn't been behaving like one for some while.

The swell raised the boat, but as it could not move under its own steam, it was thrown a hundred fathoms or two on the crest of a wave and then pitched into a trough so deep that it went out of sight for a long while.

'. . . So what do you say?' Lannec grunted, knowing that Moinard was at hand.

'Aye!'

They were both thinking the same thought, as were all the men. Lannec had taken over the wheel from the helmsman and was steering the *Tonnerre-de-Dieu* to pass as close as possible to the damaged ship so as to assess what could be done.

Seamen still had their coffee mugs in their hands. There was a smell of rum in the air, but the mugs vanished as if by magic the moment the men on board the trawler came into sight.

The *Françoise* was careening so badly that nobody could stand upright on deck. A dozen men were hanging on to the rails or the capstan, lying flat or on their haunches. They all had lifebelts, which made them look like monsters, but what was just as monstrous was the fact that they weren't moving at all. Waves crashed over the gunwales and fell on their heads and shoulders, but they didn't budge an inch as they lay there gazing at the freighter coming towards them at walking pace.

That's how they had spent the whole night, and now they probably realized themselves how difficult the rescue would be. At one point the two crews, on the *Françoise* and on the *Tonnerre-de-Dieu*, were barely fifty metres apart, and the air was clear enough to see in a flash the nervous grins of men who would maybe never be got off the wrecked ship. With furrowed brow Lannec was working out how best to manoeuvre into position when he suddenly saw a figure stand upright on the trawler. The roar of the sea prevented him from hearing anything, but to everyone on the steamer it seemed as if there was a piercing scream.

It was the cabin boy, a lanky lad with red hair. In a fit of madness, he left his position, jumped into the sea and tried to swim towards the *Tonnerre-de-Dieu*.

His face had been seen for just a few seconds before he dived, but nobody would ever forget it. They would always be able to remember his open mouth, his wild eyes and his windswept head of hair.

The men of the *Françoise* dragged themselves to the railing to see what would become of the child.

He was raised aloft for a long time by a huge wave, and there was a hope that it would be kind enough to propel him all the way to the freighter. The boy's arms flailed about. No human being had ever seemed so small and feeble.

They caught sight of him ten metres off, maybe as little as five. Three lifebuoys went over the side, and one landed within his reach.

But he could not get a hold. The wave withdrew. The lad was swept along the side of the hull into the backwash, while Lannec, now powerless, struggled to hold the rudder.

Nothing more could be done for the cabin boy! No lifeboat could survive in those seas.

'The tall fellow next to the stump of the funnel hiding his face in his hands, that's his dad,' Campois intoned. 'He already lost a son on the Grand Banks, two years ago.'

Lannec turned round and saw Mathilde standing next to Campois. She was staring straight ahead. He didn't know where she'd come from or where she'd spent the previous few hours. She was bedraggled, like everybody else, and her upper lip was swollen out of shape by an eruptive pimple.

'Émile!' she called out.

He didn't move. Once again he circled the wreck, trying to work out the best tactic.

'Émile!'

She was shivering. Her brown hair was soaked and hung in clumps over her cheeks.

'Listen to me, Émile! Let's leave! I'm scared!'

Lannec shuddered. He'd never heard those last words spoken with such a tone of voice. He was profoundly affected, as if they hadn't come from a woman, but from a mysterious, non-human voice.

'Shut up!'

'We have to leave!'

Moinard, nearby, turned his back. Campois had already taken his distance.

'Do you hear me? I do not want to die . . . Émile!'

And she screamed as she watched the great waves tipping the damaged ship ever more on its side.

'Shut your mouth!' he yelled, stamping his foot on the floor.

Was he too going to panic? He just could not stand his wife being there behind him.

'Go away!'

Then it got worse. Like the cabin boy who had jumped into the sea from terror, she lost all self-control. She grabbed the wheel, tried to turn it around to make the ship change course and bawled:

'I want to go away! I want to go home to France, don't you hear me? This ship belongs to me! You know we're going to die . . .'

'Moinard,' Lannec said in the firmest tone he could muster.

Moinard looked at the two of them and said nothing.

'Get this woman out of my way. Lock her up somewhere . . .'

But Moinard didn't budge. Mathilde, who was halfway out of her mind, bleated:

'You're murderers! Yes, all of you, murderers! You know very well we're going to die and you are doing it on purpose!'

Men on the deck raised their heads.

'I want to go away! I do! You have no right to . . .'

Seeing that his mate wasn't lifting a finger, Lannec let go of the wheel and grabbed his wife by the shoulders.

'Shut up! Come with me!'

'I want to go!'

'Of course you do. And we will, soon. But for heaven's sake, keep quiet!'

He pushed, and she pushed back, scratched his face and hands. He didn't know what to do with her. In the end, he shoved her into the chart house and bolted the door.

He was pale when he got back to the bridge and he took back the wheel, which Moinard had been handling while he was away.

'That's all we needed!' he muttered as he scanned the sea for the lost boat. To Moinard, he said:

'What do we do?'

He wasn't beyond putting a lifeboat out to sea just to get it over with, but it would be almost certain death for the men in it. Or else they could sit it out, circling the *Françoise* until the sea turned less rough. Only at this time of year, bad weather could last a week or more.

All that remained was to try one more time to get the boat in tow, but like as not the line would snap just like the one they hooked up during the night.

Lenglois appeared on the bridge with sagging shoulders and eyes bleary from exhaustion. He sighed and said:

'Fécamp is calling every ten minutes. I don't know what to tell them . . .'

Day had dawned down there as well! Léon had opened his café, the water was burbling in the percolator, and fishermen in drenched clothes were tramping in in their heavy boots.

'Stand by with the Lyle gun!' Lannec told Moinard. 'Signal the *Françoise* to stand by to receive!'

'Did you hear that?'

'Aye, aye. It's all right . . .'

He'd been hearing the noise for five long minutes already! More pieces had broken free in the hold, but tying them down was out of the question at this time. The wind was rising with the sun, and the sea was frothing.

Lenglois, for his part, was looking for Mathilde while pretending to be at a loose end. He found her at last looking out of the porthole of the chart house with her face flat against the pane.

'Murderers!' she screamed.

Lannec even felt something akin to remorse. He wanted to get it over with because he couldn't answer for what he might decide to do on the spur of the moment.

Just as when he was drowsing he almost always had two levels of awareness in his mind, one closer to a dreamscape and the other closer to the real world, he was now able to keep two trains of thought going, without realizing what he was doing.

He kept his eyes on the *Françoise* and he steered his boat with nerves of steel. But a quite different issue carried on nagging at another level of his mind.

'Whoever could have told her that?'

Because in the last analysis what had happened was the fault of the person unknown who had told Mathilde that her husband intended to resell the *Tonnerre-de-Dieu* and never return to France!

It was wrong, obviously. The idea had never crossed his mind. But his wife wasn't the one who had cooked it up . . .

Someone . . . Could it be the same person who had predicted that the *Tonnerre-de-Dieu* would never make it back to port?

He'd started suspecting everyone around him, Moinard, Monsieur Gilles, Lenglois, the bos'n, even Campois . . .

And Dame Pitard too, and that Oscar Pitard who . . .

'Standing by!' Moinard shouted from below.

Even in circumstances of this kind, Lannec could manoeuvre his boat on a sixpence, so to speak. He would stand stock still and well balanced on his short and sturdy legs, with his hands glued to the wheel and his eyes never wavering.

'Slow ahead,' he told the engine room through the speaking tube.

He got closer to the *Françoise* than he had ever dared. All men on deck held their breath and had their hearts in their mouths. Just one swirl could pitch the boats into each other.

Not one detail of what was happening on the *Françoise* went unnoticed.

'There are fifteen of them,' Campois counted. 'There should be twenty-eight.'

Fifteen men waiting for the tow-line but who had maybe

already lost faith in it. And they were shivering! They'd not had hot coffee that morning. Lannec saw one of them taking a gulp of spirits, straight from the bottle.

'Fire!'

The line made an arc in the sky like a whiplash and landed on the trawler's deck. Men crawled and scrambled to haul it in, grabbed the steel hawser and latched it on to an iron hook.

'By the grace of the Lord . . .' Lannec prayed under his voice.

It wasn't religious faith or superstition, but an old sailor's custom. He turned around to see if the cable was playing out properly and saw his wife's face hard up against the porthole.

She was screaming all on her own in a soundproof cabin!

'Dead slow ahead!' he said into the speaking tube.

Down below Mathias must have been black with oil and clinker, since he hadn't come up from the bowels of the ship for the entire night. But now and again he'd sent up a hand to get news.

The radio operator put in another appearance on the bridge.

'It's that German again . . .'

Lannec didn't stir. He had no time to lose. He calculated his course and speed to avoid making sharp tugs that would surely snap the line once again. Ironically, at that very moment, a passenger liner en route to Iceland appeared on the horizon (which was not very distant, because of the mist), unaware of the drama unfolding nearby.

'Even slower!' Lannec said into the speaking tube.

The rudderless trawler astern of the *Tonnerre-de-Dieu* was tossing like a kite in the sky that had lost its tail.

Moinard came back up. He looked at the skipper with a question in his eyes. Lannec shook his head.

It could not work! When the line went taut, it would break just like the others.

'So what then?'

'I don't know.'

The fifteen men on the deck of the trawler made a nightmarish sight, for they must have been thinking they were lost and that if the *Tonnerre-de-Dieu* moved away they had no other chance of being rescued.

'The bos'n is watching them through binoculars and says they're drinking every last drop on board.'

'Good for them!'

The line snapped at that very moment, and two tears of anger dropped from Lannec's eyes. He took his hands from the wheel and walked off a few paces.

'It's Fécamp, skipper.'

'Aye! So tell them anything you like . . . Tell them all is well, or all is ill . . .'

It wasn't any brighter at ten than at eight, and men and things were just as weighed down by the dense mass of the drizzle – the marine lung, in the words of the ancient explorer.

Sometimes a man on board the *Françoise* would wave his arms, but they'd all stopped even trying to understand what was meant.

'They're drunk,' the bos'n said.

As was the bos'n, who'd downed a whole bottle of rum on his own.

Alarm overcame the *Tonnerre-de-Dieu*'s crew as the men listened to the racket coming from the hold.

'Should I go down?' Moinard asked, pointing to the forward hatch.

'Not worth it.'

No! It wasn't worth risking men's lives in that hell where rails and axles were waltzing about without restraint.

'Listen, Moinard . . .'

He broke off and started again.

'Listen, Georges, old chum . . . You're captain as well . . .

The boat is as much yours as it is mine. If you go down, you won't come back up.'

Moinard stared hard at Lannec's clouded eyes.

'I'm going to put out in the lifeboat with one hand, a volunteer, and we'll soon see . . .'

Moinard shook his head.

'And if that's what I want to do?'

'It's not possible. I am against it. I'd rather have you tied up by your hands and feet.'

'So are we going to spend a week steaming round in circles here? We don't even have coal enough!'

By way of reply, Moinard simply looked out towards Iceland. Common sense said he was right. There was nothing that could be done. Other ships would come and wait for calmer seas to take the men off the *Françoise*, if the *Françoise* was still afloat by then.

'Your wife has shredded all the curtains.'

Like a caged dog, Mathilde had attacked everything she could get her hands on in the chart house – she'd torn up the silk curtains and the marine charts, twisted the protractor in two and spilled the bottle of calvados on the floor. Now she was lying on the bench and sobbing so hard as to make her whole body shake.

'I just can't . . .' Lannec whispered.

Then he heard a shout and turned around. As the *Tonnerre-de-Dieu* passed close by, a man had jumped off the *Françoise*, like the carrot-haired cabin boy earlier that morning. But this one was a strong swimmer.

'The lifebuoys.'

Five, then six, were thrown overboard with ropes attached. The seamen all leaned over the railing and this time the miracle happened. The sailor grasped one of the buoys and, not trusting his own strength, locked himself into it with a grimace of pain on his face.

'Haul him in gently!'

But however gently they did it he hit the hull twice over, once with his head, once with his shoulder, and when they finally laid him out on deck, he'd passed out.

It was the cabin boy's father. He had close-cropped hair on his narrow head, and his week-old beard was just as red. His breath smelled of spirits and he was bleeding from his forehead.

The other men on the *Françoise* were waving their arms as if to ask for news, and Lannec had the lights signal:

'Alive!'

He regretted doing so straight away, because it set off a mad frenzy. Another fisherman made a large sign of the cross and then jumped in.

'Starboard all!' Lannec yelled at the steersman.

And now a third man was taking his turn. Lannec's men could see them in the water and tried not to lose sight of them in the troughs.

'Buoys!'

The *Tonnerre-de-Dieu*'s hands dashed from one side of the ship to the other, but never found the man who had made the sign of the cross. The steward reckoned he'd been swept under the hull.

The third man was hanging on to a buoy, and on board the *Françoise* excitement verged on insanity. On that delirious ship men stood up, waved their arms and yelled out messages that vanished in the foaming sea and that nobody ever heard.

'Cut the engine!' Lannec ordered through the speaking tube.

It just wasn't possible to look out for all the shapes in the sea that the swell brought nearer his boat and then swept away from it. He didn't have enough lifebuoys and he didn't have enough hands.

'Starboard all, starboard, keep it to starboard, *tonnerre de Dieu!*'

'The boat's not responding . . .'

The *Tonnerre-de-Dieu* had run out of room to turn. To do so it would have to go slow ahead, and move further away from the shipwrecked men.

'One man up!' a seaman cried out as he raised a body over the gunwale.

On board the *Tonnerre-de-Dieu* they were slithering around in the wet, in confusion and doubt, and only Lannec noticed that the now abandoned wreck was closing in on her.

'Mathias, stand by! Be ready to engage the screw when I say . . .'

Mathias must have been below in the engine room. His part was to stay silent and unseen but to carry out every order that was given.

Men were running about on deck, bumping into each other and shouting out words that were lost in the tumult.

Dark shapes flailed their arms in the water. Another one rushed past as if borne on a tide and disappeared in the mist. Voices could be heard from near and far away and screams came from those still in the sea.

Suddenly, there was a sound of shattering glass. Lannec turned around and saw his wife clamber out of the chart house porthole and race madly towards the poop deck.

'Mathilde!'

She didn't hear him. Maybe she really had lost her mind? She seemed to be fleeing from danger for all she was worth, without looking back.

'Stop her!'

But there was nobody available to look out for her, as the whole crew was at the rail pulling survivors out of the water.

An intuition of disaster struck Lannec like a bolt. His ear buzzed with what she had said:

'Murderers!'

He could not leave the bridge. Everything depended on his being there. He alone was in command of the course of the *Tonnerre-de-Dieu*, which would otherwise be without power and would drift into the wreckage of the trawler.

'A few turns ahead . . .' he said into the speaking tube.

Just enough to nose forwards in the opposite direction and avoid colliding with the *Françoise*.

He couldn't see where Mathilde was. He leaned out of the door to look for her, just in time to catch sight of her climb on to the railing and jump into the sea.

'My wife! . . . Ahoy!'

A door opened, a man rushed past, and a shape went overboard. Lannec shouted:

'Stop the engines!'

The man who had jumped in after Mathilde was Lenglois. Others were hauling in two bedraggled sailors from the *Françoise* who had latched on to lifebuoys.

Lannec wasn't weeping. His eyes darted all around in dismay, but he made a superhuman effort not to abandon his post.

'A few more turns ahead . . .' he ordered.

Otherwise the hull of the trawler would hit them athwart.

As if to mock him, a voice could be heard from behind the wireless operator's open door: it was the guttural sound from the German trawler asking again and again for more news.

'Stop! Astern! Stop!'

He could make out a dense knot of people on the poop deck, then Moinard rushed up.

'Georges! Georges!' he bawled. 'Come and take over up here!'

As he strode along the deck he logged three, then four, five, seven survivors lying on the boards. One of them was already sitting up and drinking the hard liquor that Campois was feeding to him.

He stumbled over legs and feet. He found Lenglois on his knees gasping for breath with both hands crossed over his chest. Beside him lay Mathilde, with water and phlegm dribbling out of her half-open mouth. She was quite still.

10.

'Can you hear the bells?' Lannec suddenly said in a murmur when they were still a mile away from the jetty at Reykjavik.

He said it so quietly and the question was so unexpected that Jallu shivered as he turned all too sharply towards his sea-mate. All of them, from both ships, were jittery, and anything was possible.

False alarm! Lannec had his feet firmly on the deck and was checking the buoys that marked the channel into port while telling the steersman what to do. So when he talked about hearing bells, it meant that there really were bells to be heard.

They'd been steaming through the calm waters of the fjord for two hours, and dawn had broken with such a raw and lifeless light that the world seemed all blurred, as through a poorly made pane of glass. Already during the night they'd been able to make out the white caps of Iceland's mountains, but what they hadn't seen until now was that the white was streaked with black. On the peaks as on the slopes, the snow didn't entirely cover the basalt, and this irregular alternation of black and white with no halftones in between was the very picture of desolation.

'What day is it?' Lannec asked as he looked at the port through his binoculars.

All he could see were empty quays; even the streets between the steep-roofed houses were deserted. On the other hand, two, three or maybe five bell towers rang out as if in competition with each other.

'Could well be a Sunday,' Jallu sighed.

He was taller than Lannec by a head and had a drooping, straw-coloured moustache, like a Gaulish chieftain. He was wearing borrowed clothes, some from Monsieur Gilles that fitted his height but which were too narrow to button up. There were just the two of them on the bridge, alongside the steersman, who was no more alive than a machine.

'Feels like we're going into a cemetery,' Lannec went on in that gentle voice which clashed with his appearance.

Jallu shivered. For the last couple of days, the captains and the crews had all been prone to being startled for no reason, by a creak in the woodwork or a passing shadow.

'In Saint-Malo, where I come from, we have a bell like that. It's rung whenever the home fleet heaves into view . . . I can just see some black shapes in the streets now, they look like grieving relatives . . .'

He shrugged and lit his pipe, staring at Jallu with his narrow eyes, which now seemed to be seeing things a long way off.

How had he managed to understand so much in so short a time? As the hours since the incident passed by and grew into days, his fright also grew. He came to realize that he'd gone through it and seen it all as if he'd been everywhere at once.

For one thing, he would never forget the sight of Jallu sitting on deck alongside his men and propped against the rail: drenched through, without his captain's cap, with his hair plastered to his face and his moustache stuck to the week-old stubble on his cheeks, an almost unrecognizable Jallu raised himself on his hands to gaze at the *Françoise* and collapsed into convulsive weeping . . .

He sobbed uncontrollably, his chest rattled, and his wailing was so heart-chilling that it even distracted Lannec from Mathilde!

Lannec had also seen . . . Everything! He'd seen it all without wanting to. Yet he was squatting on the deck beside his wife. Liquid was still coming out of her mouth and sometimes made bubbles, which gave reason to hope. Her bodice had been torn off, and her bare breasts showed up as patches of white among so many dark-clad men.

'You must put her head down between her knees,' someone said.

She must have been dead already! They carried on trying, as Lannec looked on with bleary eyes. Heavy hands pummelled her body. Lannec had soon had enough of it.

'Leave her in peace!' he shouted as he went over to her and bent down to pick her up in his arms.

He carried her to her cabin himself, bumping into the bulkheads because of the ship's roll. It was crowded and steamy in the mess room, which was where the survivors were being given a change of clothes and a tot of rum. Lannec recalled seeing a fat, short man with chattering teeth clinging to the radiator without any clothes on at all.

It was all over. The abandoned carcase of the *Françoise* was drifting on its own on the ocean swell. Lenglois had broadcast its coordinates to all shipping and coastguards.

'You see, Jallu, it's as if you'd given an infant a glass of brandy . . . Look, the first time I went to sea, I was fifteen, I saw all the women standing on the jetty, my mother among them, and as soon as the boat started to roll in the open sea . . . I wanted to jump overboard. I struggled so hard that it took two men to hold me down . . .'

Jallu nodded politely and said nothing, but he too had a personal obsession. The two captains had been crossing paths on board for two days and said the same things to each other ten times a day.

'Your cabin boy jumped first . . . That's what made my wife

snap, like a cable under too great a strain . . . I'm not saying she was crazy, but it's much the same thing . . . Look, if you could really get to the bottom of it all, you might find she was already half crazy at the start of the voyage, when she told me about Marcel . . .'

They weren't keen on involving other people in their private conversations. They even steered clear of Moinard, who stayed as steady and silent as he ever was.

'She was a Pitard, and she was designed to live like a Pitard, in an apartment in Caen, over a shop selling shoes! . . . She'd had ideas put into her head . . . You'll see if I don't find out who did it . . .'

For two days and two nights the *Tonnerre-de-Dieu* steamed on, rocking from side to side, with some of the survivors camping out in the mess room and filling it with an acrid, barrack-room smell. Some of them hadn't said more than two words since they'd been rescued and just sat there in a daze, eating and drinking. Indeed, they all ate like lions. As if they wanted to cock a snook at death, which they'd seen so close up.

'I'd have done better to have carried on skippering other people's boats,' Jallu sometimes said with a sigh as he saw one of his hands crossing the deck.

Now it was Lannec's turn to listen and nod. Each of them was chasing his own ghost.

'What do you think they'll say, in Fécamp?'

But now it was Sunday, and the church bells of Reykjavik were summoning the faithful to worship as the *Tonnerre-de-Dieu* dawdled into port. Monsieur Gilles was at his post on the fore-castle deck. Moinard was on the landing deck wearing a heavy civilian overcoat, casting his gloomy eyes over the gloomy town.

'Believe it or not, Jallu, I have a hunch that she was beginning to love me . . . But the trouble is, she was a Pitard . . . Do you understand what I'm saying?'

He broke off and pointed to a car that had come from the town and drawn up at the quayside.

'That's for us.'

As they rounded the pier and came into the dock area, they could see there were only two other vessels at berth – an English freighter and a large mail boat.

'She got here first!' Lannec said with a wave of his hand.

He wasn't downcast. The opposite, in fact! He shrugged his shoulders to show he didn't mind. But when they'd anchored and were already steaming slow astern, he shouted:

'Is there nobody on this whole damned island?'

It was a sight to behold. The streets you could see behind the harbour were empty, and the quayside was deserted, except for the little car that had parked between the rail tracks, with occupants who had not deigned to open the door.

There wasn't anybody there to tell them which berth the *Tonnerre-de-Dieu* should take. And not even anyone to tie her up, either!

All around was that same stark contrast of black and white they'd been suffering for twenty-four hours. The only colour was in the houses, some painted pale green, others pink, but, however inexplicable it may seem, the harsh light made even those pretty colours look sad.

Just as a man was about to jump on to the quayside – at the risk of breaking a leg – someone got out of the car. He was smartly dressed, in a fur coat with an astrakhan collar and an otter-skin hat on his head, and was wearing rubber galoshes over his shoes.

As he was wearing gloves, he picked up the rope with great care so as not to get them dirty, then slipped the eye over the bollard and stood there waiting.

Lannec had not changed. He was still in his seafaring clothes, without braces or collar, with a dirty hat on his head and his coat and pea-jacket unbuttoned. Before going ashore he poured himself a tumbler of calvados and did the same for Jallu.

'Down the hatch!' he joked, unsmilingly.

Barely had the gangplank been put out than a second fur-coated man, but with a leather briefcase under his arm, emerged from the car and hurried towards the *Tonnerre-de-Dieu*.

'I'm Elbsjorn from the Electric Company, which . . .'

Elbsjorn was the first and tallest of the two characters and he spoke in English. When he got to the bridge, Lannec didn't even ask him to sit down.

'I was obliged to bring along the bailiff to certify late arrival by forty-eight hours, which means . . .'

'You can certify whatever you like,' Lannec replied in French, not bothering to switch to English.

He went to lean his elbows on the taff rail. The city wasn't entirely dead. There were people coming out of one of the wooden houses on the dockside wearing green uniforms and strange, stiff headgear.

'Customs men, or harbour police,' he thought.

In a state of apathy he fetched the paperwork from his cabin and when he got back to the bridge the police officers were already there, and they bowed with the same stiffness as the director of the electrical works.

'Can you tell me where I can get a lead coffin?'

'Ledkoffee?' queried the officer with more stripes on his arm than the others.

Lannec wasn't sure he'd used the right word in English, so he looked it up in his dictionary and underscored it with his fingernail as the policeman looked on mistrustfully.

'Tomorrow . . .' they explained. 'Today – Sunday. Not open! Not anything open!'

Survivors from the *Françoise* emerged from the mess room

dressed in ill-fitting spare clothes the crew of the *Tonnerre-de-Dieu* had lent them. Lannec smoked a pipe while the police completed the formalities.

'Where is your passenger permit?' they asked.

'My what?'

So they pointed to all the extra men on board! He didn't have the heart to get into a temper. But he didn't have the patience to explain, either. All these folk, along with the bailiff and the electrical company man, were poking their noses into his ship like rats, and suddenly, Lannec blurted out to the head of the harbour police:

'I don't have a hearse permit either!'

The shy and retreating Moinard tried to calm things down by whispering something to the officials as he pointed his chin towards the captain.

'Let them be, Georges. What do we care?'

All the same, he was obliged to change into town attire and then traipse to the harbourmaster's office and the customs post and then he called on the head of the Border Police.

'Coming with me, Jallu?'

He'd become incapable of taking a step without him, and Jallu fell in behind, wearing clothes that were too small for his girth.

There was a thin coating of ice on the black ground of the quay, and it crackled underfoot. In the town, the paving was a harsh shade of white, and it echoed like hollow stone.

The two of them saw worshippers emerge from five Protestant churches, each of a different denomination, but they didn't even turn round to look at the few women who still wore national costume with a headdress resembling a Roman helmet.

All that they noticed was a swarm of black in streets that were too white, and when they'd done with the paperwork, they sought out a café to sit in.

Unloading wouldn't start until the morning. Everything was deferred until the morning, even shore permits for the survivors of the *Françoise*.

All the cafés were shut. There wasn't even an answer when they knocked on doors. People in the street turned round to look at them and weren't shy of showing their interest in the strangers.

'What do you bet that they'll all parade along the quay to get a look?'

Lannec was right. Girls coming out of church arm in arm, lads showing off their looks, families, men in furs, just about everybody heard about the disaster of the *Françoise* and walked slowly in procession down to the quay.

'You see, Jallu, since she's a Pitard, I have to give her back to the clan . . . And yet . . .'

He didn't finish his thought, which was rather vague in any case. What he felt was a nebulous idea that if the voyage had lasted just a few days more Mathilde might have turned into a Lannec.

'She didn't really know me, you see. She was still a stranger after two years' marriage. Then some bastard told her . . .'

They espied a hotel on a newly built square in town. Lannec went into the Hekla, swung open a door on the right and saw a bar and bottles before him.

'Bring us something to drink!'

A waiter in formal attire first held back, then went to mutter something to a person in the rear, and at last came back prepared to serve them.

'If only I knew who wrote that note! I told you about it . . . It must surely be someone in the crew . . .'

They'd become old maids wittering on about bees in their bonnets, seeing nothing else in the world around them. They drank a potato spirit – *akvavit*, as it's called – and each sip made them wince, while wolfing down the slices of smoked fish they'd been served with the drink.

They were still in the bar at noon. Jallu said softly:

'We'll have to go and see the French consul about repatriation . . .'

Lannec wasn't yet drunk, but his booming voice and peremptory gestures had come back to him.

'No, Jallu! Don't do that to me! We got out of it together, and together we'll go back to Fécamp. It's for me to tell the folk back there what happened, what . . .'

He hadn't forgotten about the lead coffin and he asked the barman, who asked another customer in another room who happened to be a joiner.

'Maybe you will find someone tomorrow morning . . .'

They did not go back on board for lunch. They were determined to eat whale meat, because Lannec had had some ten years before on a port call. The hotel-keeper sent out to find some, and they didn't get to eat until two, by which time the bottle of *akvavit* was empty.

'The main thing is, don't forget my lead coffin!'

And to Jallu he said:

'Do you know what touched me the most? Her breasts. Everyone stood there looking at them. I'll tell you again, Jallu, I'll have the man who did it . . .'

When he woke up next morning unloading was in progress, and the ship agent had already been waiting for half an hour in the mess room, which still smelled like a dormitory.

All ship agents are similar. They all have the same way of speaking French, offering a cigar and spreading papers out on the table.

Lannec hadn't scrubbed up. He signed whatever was put in front of him and grunted as he lit a pipe in lieu of breakfast.

'Do you have any freight for France?'

'Dry cargo, no. But if you're looking for a deal, I've got a bargain for you: eight hundred tons of dried fish you can have for next to nothing, and which . . .'

'Jallu! Moinard!'

Now and again Lannec glanced at the door of the cabin, where his wife still lay on her bunk.

'Listen to what this fellow has to say! Turns out there's a deal to be done with some fish . . .'

He was called up to the landing deck, because a coffin was already being brought on board. He couldn't remember when he'd ordered it. In fact, the joiner from the Hekla Hotel had mentioned it to a colleague, who'd sorted it out himself.

The men on deck were staring at the waxed-pine case, which the deliverymen didn't know where to put.

'Does it have a lead lining?' Lannec shouted.

And to Campois he whispered:

'Get me a drink.'

'Milky coffee as usual?'

'Rum, you idiot!'

Just as they were about to hoist up the coffin, the customs officer ran up and stopped the crane. Lannec rushed off without changing and argued with the excise men in a great medley of languages in order to get the right permit to allow him to take his coffin with him.

But that wasn't all! He had to call on the health inspectorate as well to get a permit to export Mathilde's corpse!

People turned round in the street to look at the Frenchman, who ran into the Hekla Hotel for safety once again, where he downed several glasses of *akvavit*. He had left Jallu on board and he missed his confidant. It's true that the waiter in tails spoke French, so he got into conversation with him.

'Do you know Claridge's, in Paris? I was a waiter there for two years, around 1925 . . .'

'Have you been to Caen?'

'No, sir . . .'

In that case, nothing doing! Claridge's didn't mean a thing to Lannec! But if you knew Caen, then he could tell you all about Chandivert's, Rue Saint-Pierre, and his brother-in-law, the well-known architect.

He came across the agent when he was walking down the street.

'What did my men say about the fish?'

'They want you to decide.'

'How much?'

'You can get three banker's drafts for fifty thousand apiece and a guarantee . . .'

'Come and have a drink with me.'

He was back inside the Hekla barely after leaving it. It had already become familiar to him. He knew the bar and its glass case holding cakes topped with yellowing cream. He had his regular spot by the window and he drew the red-checked curtains closed.

'You not asking for cash in hand?'

'Just the guarantee from your bank. You can do it by wire.'

'How soon can the cod be loaded?'

'In three days' time. Tomorrow is St Peter's Day, which is a public holiday. And we won't have finished unloading. But the day after tomorrow a second team of stevedores . . .'

And that is how Lannec bought, in half-share with Moinard, 150,000 francs' worth of cod and halibut. He was living in a haze, inwardly and outwardly. Every time he caught sight of the door to his wife's cabin he went pale and felt the need of a drink.

'Jallu, old chap, I swear I'll never set foot in this miserable country again!'

Jallu had had a word with the consul, who was a shipbroker

as well, who told him that the cod that his colleague had sold wasn't worth anything at all.

The men of the *Françoise* still hadn't got shore permits and were hanging around on deck. Everyone was hanging around! Everything was going slow! They put tincture of iodine on the cuts they'd suffered when clambering up the side and which hadn't healed, because of the salt air and the cold. One of the men had got boils and was treating them rather ostentatiously in the mess room.

'There's another one nearly ripe,' he would say as he squeezed while holding a shard of mirror up to his face.

Mathilde was laid in the lead coffin and stowed in the hold, because of regulations. Lannec carried on grabbing Jallu by his buttonhole.

'I may not look like it, but I'm thinking, you see? I think on my own for hours on end. And I'm finding things out . . .'

But when he put his thoughts into words, they lost their value. The connections he saw between people and events were just too vague. When he was lying on his bunk on his own they seemed bright and clear, and he thought he could lay it all out in a few words.

'You don't know Dame Pitard! Try to imagine what she's like . . . She owns two buildings, don't you see? And a villa at Riva-Bella, which she rents out instead of staying there . . . She has a son she takes for the cleverest man on earth . . . And in the end it comes down to this: the old lady, just because she has a son, hates women, all women . . . I'm pretty sure she hated her own daughter . . .'

But that wasn't quite right, and obviously Jallu didn't understand.

'Now just suppose . . .'

It wasn't possible to explain how, but the captain was convinced that what had happened was in the last analysis a struggle between the Pitards and the Lannecs, a war between the apartment over the shoe shop in Caen and all the ships in the world that tramp from port to port!

'Who told my wife I was going to sell the *Tonnerre-de-Dieu*? Do I have that kind of reputation? No! So . . .'

And then there was the anonymous note! That's what had to be explained!

'Now, Jallu, let's suppose I'd gone down on the *Tonnerre-de-Dieu* with Mathilde . . . Dame Pitard would have inherited! Oscar Pitard would have been able to design all the workers' housing he reckoned would make him rich and famous! That's what he dreamed of . . . Apparently workers' housing projects are goldmines, because it's always easy to make money out of poor folk . . . Do you get it?'

Out on deck, in the fresh air, he didn't get it himself. He had blanks. His ideas didn't join up.

But when he was half asleep . . .

'You'll see, Jallu! I don't know your wife, but I'm telling you . . .'

A car drew up on the quay beside the boat. The consul stepped out of it.

11.

'Can you imagine that, Jallu?'

The *Tonnerre-de-Dieu* was steaming home to Normandy off the south coast of England, to avoid the north wind. Only one day out of three was foggy; they had never seen so much shipping in the Channel.

Madame Jallu told her husband by radio from the Fécamp coastguard that their eldest daughter had measles. He didn't even raise an eyebrow at the news.

He would worry about it later, when they got nearer the French coast and the life of the land would begin to mix in with the life of the sea. But when that happened he would probably worry rather more about the womenfolk waiting on the jetty who would maybe shake their fists at him.

Such things happened! Two years ago Captain Lazirec had lost an eye when a woman wanting her son back poked him with her umbrella.

Thank goodness the cabin boy's father was on board, playing cards all day long with all the others in the mess room, which had been turned into a hospital ward.

'We were wrong to go into business on our own account,' Jallu whined. 'What we're good for is sailing other people's ships . . .'

Lannec obviously wasn't listening. He was on the brink of understanding! You could go so far as to say that he'd grasped it all when the consul in that hellhole called Reykjavik had come on board.

Hadn't he come to ask if the bos'n was free of commitments and could be sent home by the Copenhagen mail boat?

'No, sir!' Lannec bawled back at the man. 'He will not leave ship. Did he ask you for permission himself?'

'He didn't ask me directly. He tried to buy a ticket, and the mail boat company asked me to check up . . .'

'You have checked up! And he will stay on the *Tonnerre-de-Dieu*!'

That was another thing that Lannec had vaguely expected. He'd often had reason to be suspicious about the bos'n ever since he'd learned that his wife told fortunes for the entire Pitard clan . . .

'Goodbye, Consul.'

He looked around for the bos'n without making it too obvious. He found him in the tiny cabin he'd made for himself in the gangway leading to the crew's quarters. He was packing his bags.

'Well, well, bos'n . . .'

Lannec shoved the man hard then upended the packed bag and shook its contents on to the floor.

There were twenty tins of lobster, no less, from the officers' stores.

'What were you doing with all that? What were you planning to cook up in Copenhagen?'

'I'm not well . . .'

'Nor am I! Everybody's ill!'

Lannec went through the swag methodically, item by item, and found another one of his own shirts, the ones he wore to go on shore.

'To make your bandages with, I presume?'

He wasn't laughing. Nor was the bos'n.

'Let's see if we can find more interesting stuff, matey . . . So what's this?'

He was holding in triumph a bottle of violet ink, one of those bottles with a twisted neck and a cap sealed with grey wax that you can get for fifty centimes in village grocery stores.

'What of it?'

'What did you use the ink for?'

Now he was sure. He didn't need any more proof. He went up to the bos'n and grabbed him by the throat.

'Confess, you bastard. It was you who put that note in the chart house! Confess it was all your doing . . .'

They could be heard in the crew's quarters, where six or seven men were dozing in their hammocks, but Lannec didn't care.

'Spill it out! What were you up to?'

He let go of the man, who rubbed his throat and rolled his eyes in fright.

'Tell me quickly, bos'n, if you don't want to get hurt! I'm in a foul mood today!'

'I didn't know.'

'What didn't you know?'

'What it would lead to . . .'

'Explain!'

'It was my wife . . .'

'Your wife what?'

'She advised Madame Pitard not to buy a boat.'

That was the Pitard clan down to a tee! Who had bought a boat? He had! He was short of 200,000 francs out of the 800,000 due, but he had a loan from the bank for that. All Dame Pitard was being asked to do was to act as guarantor of the loan, but she called it 'buying a boat' . . .

'My wife, by the way, hates the sea . . . She'd like me to do local deliveries on a bicycle . . .'

At that point the loading was just finished, and the customs officers were on board for the last pieces of paperwork. It had turned even icier that morning. Ship's radio was forecasting strong gales at sea.

'So?'

'Over the coffee grounds she told her not to be so foolish . . . Then Madame Pitard came back and said she had signed . . .'

'And then?'

'My wife wouldn't change her mind and predicted a disaster . . .'

All that had gone on in the back room of the grocery shop in Rue Saint-Pierre – presumably with a pause each time the bell rang and a customer came in at the front!

'Are you sure my mother-in-law was told there would be a disaster?'

'I swear it, so help me God!'

'Yet she let her daughter come on the voyage?'

'I think Mademoiselle Pitard – sorry, I mean Madame Lannec – had already made up her mind . . .' the bos'n stammered.

'But the old lady didn't stop her . . .'

'Not in the least!'

And he made a gesture to say there was nothing he could have done about it.

Despite being half drunk, as he had been from morning to night for the last three days, Lannec was in full control of himself and had kept a clear head, perhaps even clearer than usual, as he did when he was daydreaming.

'So Dame Pitard had "expectations" of a tragedy . . .'

'She even quizzed me as to whether a boat this old could cope with a bad storm.'

'What did you say?'

'That we'd see . . . that it was obvious the hull was rusty and that . . .'

'Wait. Let's take it in steps . . .'

Lannec didn't want to lose his train of thought.

'So, your wife foretold . . . OK! Despite which, Dame Pitard let her daughter come on board, but . . .'

He finished the sentence in his head:

'. . . but she made me sign a will leaving everything to the surviving spouse and had me take out life insurance for . . .'

'Shut up!' he yelled at the bos'n, who had only just opened his mouth.

'Why did you sign on for this voyage?'

'Because I didn't want to be a delivery cyclist . . . I've done twenty-eight years on sailing vessels and ten years on steam . . .'

Lannec didn't even smile.

'Except that you wrote me a note . . .'

It was the bos'n's turn to go red in the face.

'Why?'

'To keep you alert.'

'I don't understand.'

'The coffee grounds said . . .'

'Eh? Do you believe in that stuff?'

'How can you know?' the bos'n muttered.

'Do you get it, Jallu, my old mate! His wife sells fortunes, but he's not sure he doesn't believe them as well . . . He dresses up as a ghost to steal a ham, but in Hamburg he buys mumbo-jumbo to recite when putting ointment on his scald . . . There's only Dame Pitard . . .'

But those weren't things she could say. She had scarcely even thought them, except she did them all the same, telling herself that things would turn out as they would.

What use did she have for a daughter married to a ship's captain? And not just any captain! Every time he was on shore the fellow tried to prove he was cleverer than her own son, a Pitard and a learned man!

'Since you insist on going on the voyage with your husband, so be it, and the worse for you! But perhaps you are right. Now he has the ship and our signature, he's quite capable of never coming back . . .'

There are no doubt true facts in mathematics. When Lannec computed the angle of a star, he was confident he would get it right. But on this issue, he was surer than sure!

'But has he even made any arrangements? Are you sure that if anything happened to him his mother wouldn't come and have the boat sold so as to retrieve her share in the inheritance?'

Because Lannec's mother was part of the story. He gave 600 francs a month to the old lady in a Breton bonnet who lived in a hovel in Paimpol.

The Pitard clan was up in arms. Six hundred francs a month which . . .

So that explained the life insurance business.

'Listen to me, bos'n. I'm stopping myself from smashing your face in, but . . .'

But the bos'n was another story. After thirty-eight years of service at sea, he had a wife who wanted to send him out on a bicycle to deliver vegetables. He was pitiful! He lowered his head in shame.

'Do you really believe in that nonsense?'

The bos'n said nothing but pointed to a horseshoe that had fallen out of his bag.

'I wanted to warn you . . .'

He was still lying a little bit. What he'd wanted most of all was to give him a scare, just like he'd scared Campois, so as to allay his own fears.

'You are a piece of scum!' Lannec told him seriously as he left the man's messy lair.

He hadn't even laid his hand on the bos'n's face.

'You see,' he said to Jallu. 'You can be your own boss if you've got the wherewithal. But what you mustn't do is . . .'

He blushed and gave an order to the steersman, unnecessarily, just to have something to do.

'All the same, if it hadn't happened so quickly . . .'

He recalled the sound of Mathilde's voice and the look in her eyes when she'd stood behind him and said:

'Émile! . . . Listen to me, Émile! Let's leave! I'm scared!'

The trouble was, she was a Pitard, and he hadn't listened.

For in spite of all the Marcels at Chandivert's and her architect brother . . .

'I'm going to tell you something you mustn't ever repeat . . . Just between the two of us, right, till the grave takes us both. Well, the fact is that now, at present, I'm in love with that . . .'

That . . . that . . . that what?

He could see the water dribbling out of her mouth like a real sailor's lost at sea, and the deckhands pummelling her chest not because there were female breasts on it but because they hadn't given up trying to bring her back to life . . .

'Maybe she was worth more than me, Jallu, and it's all the fault of her wicked mother . . .'

When the time came to throw spades of earth into her grave in the cemetery in Caen people realized that Lannec had vanished. To keep up appearances, Dame Pitard took the spade firmly in her hand and gave it to her son.

'There will be a private and informal dinner at home,' she made it known to a few relatives and friends, while the others stood and waited for the bus at the cemetery gate.

Lannec, who had a cold and was wearing a collar that was too high and stiff for his neck, sat on his own at Chandivert's in the seat where he'd first set eyes on Mathilde.

By chance the band was playing the 'Blue Danube' waltz,

which reminded him of Honningsvåg and the pretty Hungarian girls . . .

Suddenly the violinist caught sight of the sailor in mourning dress. The music stopped for a second, then raced ahead to catch up with itself.

Marcel had panicked! His terrified gaze had been looking for support and had found it, once more, in Lannec, who made a gesture with his hands as if to say:

'Don't be afraid . . .'

The skipper was pale, and his eyes were red. The bowler hat he had bought for the occasion did not fit his head.

But as he nodded to the beat his head kept on saying:

'Don't be scared. Don't worry, I won't hurt you.'

What could he have done to a wretch like that in any case?